SECOND IN THE

DUTCH FREEDOM
S E R I E S

Open the Dikes

REBECCA MARTIN

ISBN: 978-1-890050-03-0

Rebecca Martin
Cover by Joyce Hansen and Grace Martin
Book Design by: Larisa Yoder
Printed in the USA by Carlisle Printing of Walnut Creek

Carlisle Press
WALNUT CREEK

2673 Township Road 421
Sugarcreek, Ohio 44681
phone | 800.852.4482

Titles in the

DUTCH FREEDOM
S E R I E S

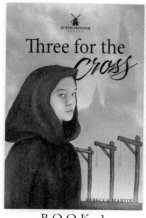

B O O K 1

B O O K 2

Coming soon!

Lord
Of The
Sea

B O O K 3

Coming soon!

Out of
Egypt

B O O K 4

Foreword

The main characters in Book 2 of the Dutch Freedom series are mostly fictional. Only Hansken and Bettgen Vervest, who were also mentioned in Book 1, are found in the chronicles of history. All the political characters, of course, are factual, including their names and their major doings. All place names are real for that time period, though some are different today. The events of the Dutch Revolt are entirely based on fact. That remarkable occurrence at Leiden really happened.

Bibliography

Mennonite Encyclopedia

Encyclopedia Britannica

World Book

William of Orange, The Silent Prince by WG Van de Hulst (first printed 1992)

The Revolt of the Netherlands by Pieter Geyl (first printed 1932)

Rebecca Martin

· Open the Dikes ·

Table of Contents

Part One
Gerrit

chapter one

Aboard the Hollander

G errit Lieven yawned. Life as a Sea Beggar could certainly be boring—especially when the weather was nice and the North Sea remained smooth as glass for days on end. When had the *Hollander* last seen action? Why, it was weeks since they'd captured the last Spanish merchant ship.

Stifling another yawn, Gerrit glanced across the deck at Jules. The young boatswain leaned against the ship's second mast. "You look just as bored as I feel," Gerrit told him.

Jules scowled. "Things are too quiet for me. Why don't we just rise up and drive the Spanish out of the Netherlands, once and for all?"

"I know what you mean," Gerrit agreed. "Last October I had high hopes, when Prince William of Orange actually came in with an army and attacked the Spanish. Then his attack turned into a spectacular failure, badly disappointing us Sea Beggars. We look to William as our leader—but where is he right now? Why, back in Germany, nursing his wounds."

Jules shook his head dolefully. "I never could figure out William of Orange. The Dutch people want him. He could lead us to freedom. But he's so cautious. On the one hand, he tries to please the Dutch; on the other hand, he still wants to please King Philip of Spain. He'll never get anywhere if he keeps a foot in each camp."

"If we could only chase out the Duke of Alba!" Gerrit said grimly. "I wonder if King Philip knew, when he made Alba governor of the Netherlands, what a cruel man he is. He's killing hundreds of so-called heretics—and taking pleasure in it. No doubt he would gladly kill every last one of us Sea Beggars too."

Jules grinned. "He won't catch us. But Gerrit, this reminds me of something I've wanted to ask. Where did we get this name of 'Sea Beggars'? We're not poverty stricken or anything. Our captain is a wealthy nobleman, and we sailors live in high style."

"I guess you're pretty young," Gerrit remarked sardonically. "The name 'Sea Beggars' goes back to 1566, before the days of Alba, when Margaret of Parma was still governess of the Netherlands. At the time, King Philip was tightening his control, putting Spanish bishops in charge of the Catholic churches and persecuting the Protestants. Some Dutch noblemen got together and approached Margaret, petitioning her to relax the persecution. Because of that petition, the noblemen were given the nickname of 'Beggars.' A rather derisive name, but nobody seems to mind."

Jules pulled idly at a rope dangling from the mast. "That's what I find hard to understand. For our ensign we have a chain and a cup—symbols of poverty and begging—yet we seem to take a perverse sort of pride in these symbols."

"Oh well, I guess we could be called worse names." Gerrit shrugged. "When Alba came into the Netherlands, a lot of the nobles who'd petitioned Margaret fled the country. But later some came back as guerrilla warriors, making forays against the Spanish. On land, the fighters were called 'Wild Beggars;' and we on the ships are 'Sea Beggars.'"

Jules stared unhappily at the green wavelets sliding beneath the ship's bow. "Seems to me we haven't accomplished very much in these years. All we've done is plunder a few towns and capture a few Spanish ships. We're acting like pirates—all in the name of religion. The glorious, Reformed, Calvinist religion!" Sarcasm dripped from his voice. Then, suddenly, he gave Gerrit a strange look. "Are you a Calvinist, or are you not?"

"Don't blame you for wondering," Gerrit responded with a wry grin. "No doubt you've noticed that I don't take an enthusiastic part in the on-board worship. To tell you the truth, Jules, I'm nothing. Not Calvinist, not Lutheran, not Catholic. No religion at all."

Amazement flooded Jules's features. "You weren't baptized as a baby?"

"Nope. You see, my parents were Mennonite."

The word seemed to drop like a cannonball on Jules. "Mennonite!" he exploded. "Yet here you are, on a pirate ship, happily fighting the Spanish! I thought it's only the Calvinists who do that."

"Not just. After my parents were slain, I was—well, set adrift. I didn't know what to do. Joining the Beggars gave me a purpose in life." Hunching his shoulders, Gerrit gazed at the hazy shoreline barely visible on the horizon. Why had he told this to the young boatswain, anyway? Up to now his early days had been a well-kept secret. No one on the ship had cared enough to ask.

"Your parents got killed, you said. Like—burned at the stake for being heretics?"

Swallowing hard, Gerrit nodded. Most of the time he diligently herded his thoughts away from such memories. Jules's forthright questions were opening up raw wounds.

"And they didn't have you baptized as a baby?" Jules looked him over wonderingly, as though he were an extreme oddity.

Curtly, Gerrit replied, "Surely you know why the Mennonites are also called Doopsgezinde. They have this big thing about needing to grow up and be accountable before you're baptized. My parents believed that strongly. Much good it did their children, though. I was only fourteen when they—when they were taken. My sister was twelve. The Catholics had her baptized as soon as they'd killed my parents. Elsa's in Antwerp now, married to a wealthy Catholic merchant."

"Antwerp. We're not far from there right now, are we?" Jules asked. "Up ahead is the estuary of the Scheldt River. Antwerp's only—what is it?—fifty miles up the Scheldt."

"Uh-huh." Gerrit turned to fix his eyes on Jules. "What about you? You look young enough to still be living with your parents. What brought you to the wild sort of life?"

Jules's face reddened. "My father was too strict. Have you any idea how strict a Calvinist can be? I ran away because I couldn't take it anymore."

"Hmm. So you're not exactly a good Calvinist either."

"I never said I was." Jules's voice had turned defensive. Suddenly his arm shot out, pointing toward the horizon. "A ship! It's got a Spanish ensign. I wonder if our lookout—"

Just then a shout rang out from above. In response, the entire crew sprang into action. Sails were trimmed for improved maneuvering. Guns were primed and loaded. Rowboats were readied for swift deployment. Captain Reynard had trained his men well. Everyone knew exactly what he must do to help capture an enemy ship.

Approaching the Spanish ship, the *Hollander's* guns opened fire. Flames raked the victim's port side. Only a few answering shots rang from the Spanish ship.

Soon the command came to board the enemy ship. This was where Gerrit's expertise came into play. Along with selected crew members, he helped put boats over the side. Swiftly rowing across the intervening water, they soon boarded the Spanish ship by means of grappling irons.

Up over the railing struggled Gerrit. Suddenly a sharp pain knifed between his shoulder blades.

In that instant Gerrit Lieven's world went black.

· Open the Dikes ·

chapter two

The Sister Who Cared

L ight drummed on Gerrit's eyelids, pulsing, throbbing.
"Wake up! The darkness is past. It's time to get going," the
light seemed to say.

Slowly, painfully, Gerrit forced his eyes open. There above him
was a vision of a lovely face. A woman's face, with deep blue eyes,
golden hair, and a beaming smile. Why did the face look vaguely
familiar?

"Well, Gerrit, you're awake!" The woman beamed some more
as she adjusted his pillow. "Here, shall I help you sit up? You are
looking quite well this morning. Better than you have for weeks."

"Weeks?" he repeated groggily. "Have I been sick or something?"
A dull pain nagged at his back as the woman drew him into a
sitting position.

She chuckled. "Have you been sick? Well, I should say so.
It started when you had a run-in with a Spaniard's sword.
Remember? You were boarding a Spanish ship. Just climbing over

the railing when this Spaniard came along with his sword. You fell into the rowboat and were taken back to the *Hollander*. At first they thought you were dead. Come, Gerrit. Surely you can recall climbing up those grappling irons?"

He nodded, remembering the feel of his hands grasping the chains. "And yes, there was a sharp pain…"

"That's when you blacked out." She patted his hand. "Once the sailors realized you weren't dead, they didn't know what to do with you. Fortunately there was a young boatswain who knew that you have a sister in Antwerp. So they brought you here to recover."

Gerrit jerked his head back to stare at her face. "You're my sister? Elsa?"

"That's me all right," she responded cheerily. "I was beginning to wonder when you'd ever recognize me. I know, it's been a few years since we met, but surely I haven't changed that much."

"No. No. You haven't changed; it's just that my mind seems befuddled." He lay back, memories of the past flooding his thoughts. Memories of the weaver's cottage where the two of them had lived with their parents near a small village in the province of Groningen. Memories of a cow, a pig, and a horse named Rippert, which was used to till their small patch of land.

In spite of the pain knifing him, Gerrit turned to look at his sister, who busied herself at the other side of the room. "Elsa. Do you ever have any regrets? I mean, wondering how it would be if—if things hadn't gone the way they did?"

She came over and sat beside the bed. "Of course, I sometimes wonder. But I have a nice life now. Whereas with the Mennonites— well, they have no future. Not with Alba persecuting them so fiercely."

"I used to like going to meetings with Father and Mother," Gerrit said dreamily.

His sister admitted, "So did I. Those people—well, they loved each other. It was a brotherhood. You don't get that with the Catholics. Not really."

"Must be something about Mennonitism…something that really takes hold on you. Else why would people give their lives for it?" Gerrit was surprised at himself for expressing his thoughts so freely to this sister whom he barely knew.

Elsa looked thoughtful. "From what Father and Mother used to say, I'm guessing it's not actually Mennonitism that holds them. It's Jesus. He was—He was so real to Father and Mother."

"That must be it," Gerrit agreed. "I can't imagine giving my life for a man named Menno Simons. But Jesus—He's God's Son. I can still hear the minister saying, 'Love is the truest mark of the followers of Jesus.'"

"Fancy you remembering that." She gave his hand another sisterly pat. "I never knew you could be so philosophical. Must be the weeks of delirium that changed you."

"Weeks," he said again, mulling over the thought. "I must have been pretty sick. It's like I lost a chunk out of my life, a chunk without any memories. If it hadn't been for you, I probably wouldn't have survived."

"I'm glad we could help you." She wiped a tear from her cheek.

His tone turned gruff. "You wouldn't have been obligated. I've never done a thing for you."

"Well, there's this thing about love," she reminded him. "Maybe our early teaching paid off. How could I have said no when they brought you to our door?"

He shook his head and repeated, "You weren't obligated."

A light tap sounded on the bedroom door. "That'll be the children," said Elsa, hurrying to open.

"Tryntgen! Ghysbrecht! Uncle Gerrit is awake and eager to see you," she greeted them.

Golden-haired and blue-eyed like their mother, a boy and a girl came hesitantly up to the bed. Their shy smiles went straight to Gerrit's heart. "So you're my niece and nephew. I haven't seen you in a long while; not since you were babies. But I guess you must have been seeing me before I saw you, while I lay here like a man who can't wake up."

That made them chuckle. As though he'd wanted for weeks to ask his question, Ghysbrecht began, "Did you like being a Sea Beggar, Uncle Gerrit?"

He shrugged. Somehow he knew right away that he did not want to make the pirate life sound glamorous to this impressionable young boy, his sister's precious son. "It was something to do, I guess."

Ghysbrecht was visibly disappointed. "I thought it must be fun on a ship."

"It's okay, I guess. But kind of dangerous, as you can see," he added wryly.

From the corner of his eye he noticed Elsa stealing from the room. She probably had no idea that it gave him a panicky feeling to be left alone with his niece and nephew. He'd had so little to do with children.

Still, these two seemed rather easy to converse with. Tryntgen, who appeared to be the older of the two, had a question of a different sort to ask. "Mother says Grandpa and Grandma Lieven were Mennonites. Does that mean you are a Mennonite too?"

"No. You see, Mennonites don't baptize their babies, so you

don't become one just by being born into a Mennonite family, the way it is for Catholics or Calvinists." Surprised by his own ready reply, Gerrit wondered what the maiden would ask next.

He had not long to wait. "How do people become Mennonites then?" she persisted.

Gerrit thought fast. "Well, you might say it's a choice. A person has to grow old enough to—to choose. Then if he decides to, he can be baptized into the Mennonite faith."

She giggled. "Imagine baptizing a grown person! How could the priest handle him?"

Realizing she pictured a baby in the arms of a priest, Gerrit chuckled too. "There are different ways of baptizing people. I remember a Mennonite baptismal service from when I was young. The people knelt on the ground, and the minister poured water on their heads. But first they had to answer some questions and make some promises."

"Oh. Because they'd made a choice," Tryntgen said wisely.

Ghysbrecht piped up, "Isn't it dangerous, being a Mennonite?"

"In a way, yes." Feeling suddenly tired, Gerrit sank back into his pillow.

As if by magic, Elsa appeared with an exclamation: "You children are tiring Gerrit with your questions. He should rest now. If he wants you to, you can come back some other time."

She herded the two from the room, while Gerrit's thoughts went far into the past, to a day at school. A classmate had asked a question similar to Ghysbrecht's: "Isn't it scary to be Mennonites?"

Gerrit had responded with a question of his own. "Why would it be scary?"

"Well, my father was saying how a bunch of Mennonites over at Ipsheim were captured at a meeting. And they're all in jail now!"

Hands on hips, Gerrit's classmate had stood there, awaiting an answer to his original question.

Gerrit's cousin—also the son of Mennonites—had come to his rescue. "It's not too bad if you have a nice magistrate, like we do here in our village."

At a young age, therefore, Gerrit had learned what a difference it made if the area's magistrate was inclined to deal leniently with "heretics." Since their magistrate's wife actually herself belonged to the Doopsgezinde, it wasn't hard to understand why he favored them.

Over the years, however, things had gradually changed. The Mennonites began holding their meetings at night, out in the forest. When Gerrit asked why, his parents explained that higher authorities were putting a lot of pressure on the magistrate, demanding that he capture all Mennonites.

For a boy, of course, secret nighttime meetings had been kind of fun—as long as they weren't discovered. Gerrit remembered vividly the first time that had happened. Even all these years later, his heartbeat still quickened as he recalled the breathless flight through the dark forest.

chapter three

Parable of the North Sea

Lying there waiting for his wounds to heal, Gerrit had hours of time to think, hours of time to recall the past. Sometimes the memories became so vivid that it seemed he was right there, experiencing things all over again...

"Menno Simons is coming!" Happy whispers spread the news through the Mennonite community. The elder did not often come to this village. When he did, there were numerous baptisms and marriages waiting to be performed, besides the communion service to which everyone looked forward.

Gerrit's father explained, "It's not easy for Menno to visit the Netherlands. He is very much hated by the Dutch authorities."

"Doesn't Menno live in the Netherlands? I thought he was born not far from here," Gerrit said in surprise.

"He taught and baptized in these provinces for a number of years. But his life was constantly in danger here, so he now lives in the German province of East Friesland, near Holstein," Father replied.

Gerrit was puzzled. "But isn't it Emperor Charles who hates us so much? I thought Charles rules over East Friesland just as much a he does over Groningen."

Father nodded. "Supposedly, Charles is also emperor over the German provinces. But he hasn't nearly as much power there, because the local princes are often Lutheran. They dare to resist the Catholic emperor. Many of them are quite lenient towards the Mennonites."

"Then why don't we move to Germany too?" Elsa wondered.

Father's face turned serious. "We have thought of it. But there is the language problem to consider. Are you ready to learn German, Elsa?"

She shrugged. "If Menno could, I suppose I could too. I'm tired of being in danger all the time."

Mother sighed. "For your sakes, we would certainly like to live in a more peaceful spot."

Gerrit put in soberly, "Some people get killed for being Mennonites."

"I know." Briskly, Father changed the subject. "We must get our little house ready to host Menno. He is coming here tonight, after the meeting. Early in the morning, I'm to take him down the canal to Rueysbaek."

"Are you taking Uncle Wouter's boat? Can I go too?" Gerrit asked eagerly.

Father's eyes met Mother's, then turned to Gerrit. "I suppose you may come. It will mean rising before dawn, though."

Evening came at last. Shivering with excitement, Gerrit walked with Father, Mother, and Elsa deep into the forest. He knew the spot: an open glade, but well hidden by the surrounding trees. And in case the bailiffs were to surprise them, those same trees would save at least some of the congregation as they fanned out into the dark forest.

It was an eventful evening—eventful, but peaceful. Midnight arrived by the time they had celebrated communion, witnessed several marriages, and watched sixteen people receive baptism. Though Gerrit didn't know Menno Simons very well, it seemed to him that the elder looked weary as he entered the Lievens' house and accepted the bed they offered him.

Only a scant few hours later, Father was shaking Gerrit awake. "Do you still want to come along on the trip down the canal?"

That brought him wide awake. Taking some food Mother had prepared for them, the three stole through the pre-dawn darkness to the canal. How peaceful it seemed at this time of day! The water lay mirror-smooth under the dark sky. Reflected stars twinkled from the surface. Dip-splash, dip-splash went the oars as Father and Menno each took one. Past barns and houses they slid, past windmills creaking to life with dawn's first breezes, past wide flat polders where cows grazed contentedly. In spite of the danger, in spite of the awareness that they were transporting a hunted man, these early-morning hours were fastened in Gerrit's memory as some of his life's most peaceful. Father and Menno talked quietly all the way down the canal, about God, about Jesus, about His saving power and guiding love.

It was the last time the Lievens saw Menno Simons. That day at noon, a neighbor—not a Mennonite, but a sympathizer—came breathlessly to their door. "You should flee! The bailiffs found out that Menno was here. They are going around questioning people. Anybody who gave food or shelter to Menno is in danger." The neighbor paused to catch his breath. "Your life is in danger! The bailiffs mean business. Aiding Menno in any way is considered an offense worthy of death."

Gerrit never forgot that moment: how Mother's face turned pale, while Father calmly thanked the neighbor. After he had gone, Father turned to Mother and said, "I believe the time has come."

Mother nodded. And although they did not say it in so many words, Gerrit understood what they meant. It was time to flee from the province of Groningen.

"Where will we go?" The words burst unbidden from Gerrit's lips.

"To Antwerp, in Flanders," Father told him, thus revealing that they had long been planning for this moment.

"And we won't be persecuted there?" That was Elsa's anxious question.

"No guarantees," Father admitted. "But there are many brethren in Antwerp—thousands, even. Calvinism is gaining ground over Catholicism in parts of the city, which means the Catholics' power is limited. So we have hopes we can live and worship in peace there."

"Haven't I heard people calling Antwerp the 'weavers' city'?" asked Gerrit.

"Perhaps you have," answered Father with a smile. "But it could just as well be called the tailors' city, or the printers' city, or just about any other trade. Europe has no greater industrial center than Antwerp."

Dinner over, Gerrit downed his last bite of bread. "Then I guess you'll like the city, if there are lots of weavers." Over the years he'd become aware that Father was not first and foremost a farmer, but a weaver. Farming was merely a way to raise food for the family; weaving was how Father supported the family.

"So we'll be city people," Elsa said dolefully. She, more than anyone in the family, liked the farm work.

Father sprang to his feet. "Here we sit, talking! We must go. Now. I've made arrangements with neighbor Jakob; he is set to buy this place whenever I say the word. Mother, you'll remember which things we planned to take."

Gerrit and Elsa could only watch in amazement as their parents set in motion the plans they had kept secret until now. Before noon the family was in Uncle Wouter's boat, heading along canals toward the North Sea.

"I'd have thought we'd wait till after dark," Elsa fretted. "Everyone will see our boat."

"It's not very convenient for the bailiffs to stop boats," Father reminded her. "But if you like boating at night, we'll get plenty of that before we reach Antwerp."

The excitement of reaching the North Sea made Gerrit forget the danger they were in. "All that water!" he exclaimed, surveying the choppy waves stretching to the horizon. "It makes the coastal dikes seem rather puny, to think they're holding back a sea this size."

"You remind me of something brother Jan van Claeve once mentioned in a sermon," Father said. "He compared God's 'river of water of life' to the North Sea—boundless, vast, always flowing. 'Yet we humans tend to build dikes around our hearts and lives,' Jan said. 'We shrink from surrendering completely to God's flow of life. But why do we torment ourselves so? Why do we not simply open our hearts through repentance and allow the divine life to flood every corner of our beings?'"

Although Gerrit nodded in assent, he did not really understand what Father was saying. Many times Gerrit had questioned why his parents chose to live in danger as "heretics" when they could have had a comfortable existence in the state church. But this parable of the North Sea showed him that his parents were claimed by something far greater than themselves. They lived and moved, not as individuals in control of their own lives, but as part of a vast entity that carried them irresistibly toward eternity. Now Gerrit knew a name for that entity: God's "river of water of life"—boundless as the North Sea.

They spent a day and a half with friends of Father's on the coast until he managed to arrange transport on a ship heading south. Seasickness took some of the joy out of that trip; yet as the ship traveled up the Scheldt River toward Antwerp, Gerrit felt sorry that the voyage would soon be over. There was something about the sea…

To these country dwellers from the northern provinces, Antwerp was breathtaking. Buildings crowded the Scheldt's banks. Soaring cathedral spires pierced the sky. Freighter ships thronged the harbor. Wide-eyed with wonder, Elsa whispered, "Now I see why we can be safe in this city. It's so big we can disappear in it."

"Lord willing," said Father, "we can stay together and find fellowship here, while our children grow up to serve the Lord in truth."

"Look at that castle!" exclaimed Gerrit, pointing to ramparts and towers of stone that loomed high on the riverbank.

"If I have it correct, this castle is called the Steen," Father told him.

Tipping back his head, Gerrit viewed the tallest tower. "Do you think anyone lives in this castle?"

Father shook his head. "Not likely. At least, no one's living there by choice. Nowadays the old castles that were built in the 1300s and 1400s are mostly used as prisons."

"So for all we know, some Mennonites are in the Steen right now as prisoners," Gerrit said somberly. The thick walls and barred windows looked somehow forbidding.

Elsa wondered, "What were castles used for years ago?"

"They were homes built for royalty," Mother told her. "Maybe some kings and princes still live in such old castles, but I'm sure modern houses offer more comfortable living quarters."

Father put in, "Castles also used to serve as fortresses. During times of war people took refuge in them. But castles are no match for the cannons and gunpowder that are used these days."

Since Father had made numerous trips to Antwerp in the past, he knew the way to a friend's home. They were greeted with the warmest hospitality, and with assurances that a small house could easily be bought. For now at least, life in Antwerp looked promising.

· Open the Dikes ·

chapter four

The Basest of Men

B ut the Lieven family had reckoned without Titelman. No one had told them about this Catholic dean who had been made official inquisitor of Flanders. Like Saul of Tarsus, Pieter Titelman went "breathing out threatenings and slaughter against the disciples of the Lord." Obstinate and hard-hearted, Titelman's all-consuming passion was to destroy heretics. Although much of his hated work was done in the surrounding towns, by now the long arm of Titelman's law also began to reach Antwerp.

The church adapted. Instead of having large meetings, numerous small meetings were held throughout the city, or even outside in the forest. Often the meetings started early in the morning, so that the brethren could travel the streets before dawn. Then they would stay all day, not daring to venture out until darkness had fallen again.

However, like bloodthirsty police hounds, Titelman's bailiffs sometimes caught their prey. Gerrit was thirteen on the day he found out what it was like when a meeting is interrupted by bailiffs. One moment the brethren were reverently singing psalms; the next moment, doors were flung open and cruel-faced men burst in with chains at the ready.

Since the brethren far outnumbered the police, not everyone was caught. The entire Lieven family managed to escape. Having reached home with no one in pursuit, they sat there catching their breaths and looking relieved.

"God must still have a purpose for us here on earth," Father said quietly.

The words sent a chill through Gerrit. Obviously, Father lived with the constant awareness that life could end any moment.

How Gerrit's heart rebelled at the thought! Every day, he worked at Father's weaving shop, learning the trade. If Father were suddenly gone, he was by no means ready to continue alone. He needed Father.

Unaware of Gerrit's thoughts, Father went on, "I noticed a bailiff putting chains on Claes den Koop, the brother who kept us until we were able to buy a house here in Antwerp. I'm going to make inquiries. If they put him into the Steen dungeon, I might look him up."

"You mean you could actually visit him in prison?" Gerrit asked in surprise.

"Not exactly. But the dungeon cells have windows. I've heard of brethren who encouraged prisoners through the bars."

Elsa clasped her hands. "I hope you take care, Father."

"We are always in God's care, Elsa—no matter what happens," Father assured her.

Gerrit stared gloomily at the wooden floor. He had a hard time believing so implicitly in God's care. If God was so powerful, why did He not stop this terrible persecution? Why were men like Pieter Titelman allowed to wreak havoc among God's followers? There were so many questions.

Elsa must have harbored some of the same questions. She burst out, "I thought we came to Antwerp because it's supposed to be safer here! Now look what's happening. The police are always after us. Why didn't we just stay in Groningen?"

"My child, I don't have answers for all your questions," Father admitted. "But we felt it was God's leading to come here, so that is what we did."

"It's like—like we just don't have a future," Elsa stormed, even while tears ran down her cheeks.

"Things may change soon," Mother soothed. "I heard that Charles V no longer wants to be emperor. That should make a difference for the Mennonites. Charles was the one who passed edicts making us outlaws worthy of death."

"So Charles can just quit being emperor?" Gerrit asked curiously.

"Apparently. He's retiring to a monastery somewhere in Spain." Getting to her feet, Mother stirred up the flames in the fireplace. "Charles's son Philip will now be king of Spain—but he won't be Holy Roman Emperor. I don't know what we can expect from Philip. Many people in the Netherlands would be very happy to see the end of Spanish rule."

"But Margaret of Parma is still our governess, and she hates us too," Elsa muttered.

Father said firmly, "We must commt it all into God's hands. He rules the universe."

By the following week, Father was successful in his plan to find Claes den Koop. Having spent most of the night away, Father recounted his adventures the next morning.

"Getting lost in the forest was the hardest part," he began with a twinkle in his eyes. "I'd thought the directions given me were fairly simple. The brethren know an underground way to exit the city; I found that easily enough. And I'd been told it's only a short trek through the forest till you reach the Steen. Well, I must have gone around in circles, because it took me over an hour to find the castle. Then, of course, I had to find the correct window. I bungled that too. I'd been told de Koop's is the fourth one from the northwest corner, so I groped my way through the darkness to what I thought was the right one. Peering through the bars, I called his name as loudly as I dared. Suddenly a woman's voice answered me! She sounded quite annoyed. I must have woken her up.

"By that time I felt quite befuddled. I groped along the castle wall until I realized I'd started counting at the wrong corner. Finally I found the correct window—and Claes answered my call right away. I was relieved, to say the least." Father sighed. "We talked for hours. Claes related how Pieter Titelman himself sometimes comes in to question the prisoners. He is very sharp, and often quotes Scriptures to support what he's saying. Claes said he felt greatly intimidated by Titelman's cruel ways. Without God's help he would have been unable to say a word.

"The strangest part of that interview was this: at one point, Titelman actually admitted that the Mennonites' conduct is irreproachable. He said people everywhere praise them for their peace, love, and charity. Yet this is how he summed things up: 'But what is the good of all that, if you don't have the right faith?'"

Gerrit couldn't help smiling. "So apparently you can be as wicked as you like, just as long as you're Catholic. But if you're Mennonite, no amount of goodness can make you okay."

"It seems that is Titelman's theory," Father agreed. "He is a very obstinate man, and will listen to no one who tries to make him think otherwise."

Elsa wailed, "Why does God allow such people to rule?"

Father stared thoughtfully into the fire. "Elsa, have I ever told you the account in the Bible of how Daniel interpreted a dream for the king of Babylon?"

Elsa slumped sullenly onto the bench. "Not that I can recall."

"Being king of Babylon in those days must have been a lot like being Holy Roman Emperor today. This King Nebuchadnezzar was very powerful. But he found his dream disturbing. In it he saw a tree grow tall and flourishing. Then a holy one came from heaven and said that the tree must be hewn down. This holy one spoke some words to the king that we still believe today: *The most High ruleth in the kingdom of men, and giveth it to whomsoever he will, and setteth up over it the basest of men* (Dan. 4:17). Elsa, God's ways are so much higher than ours. It is simply not in our place to question Him, and wonder why certain men are allowed to rule."

In his corner near the hearth, Gerrit pondered those words: "He setteth up over it the basest of men." Certainly Pieter Titelman sounded like the "basest of men."

Father continued his story. "As you know, Daniel was a God-fearing man. He prayed for help to interpret the dream, and this is what he told the king: 'You are that flourishing tree. You will be cut down, and lose your empire. For some years you will be little more than a beast, but later your kingdom will be restored.' And Elsa, things happened just as Daniel had said. That's how powerful God is. Believe me, the 'Most High still ruleth in the kingdom of men', and we may trust Him in complete confidence."

· Open the Dikes ·

chapter five

Off to the Sea

Still the terrible persecution raged on in Flanders, under King Philip no less than under Charles V. If anything, Philip seemed even more intent upon ridding his lands of heretics. No inquisitor was too cruel or implacable for Philip's purposes.

Many brethren were fleeing from Antwerp now—and ironically, many of them went to the northern provinces from which the Lievens had come. "Couldn't we go back too?" Elsa pleaded early one morning as the family prepared to leave for worship. "Maybe Jakob would even sell our farm to us again. Maybe—maybe he still has dear old Rippert!"

Father looked at her with kind, yet troubled, eyes. "It seems you haven't forgotten our old plowhorse. Elsa, we are praying about these things, but so far we have not felt led to leave Antwerp."

Gerrit heard his sister mutter something under her breath. Though he couldn't be sure, it sounded very much as though she'd said, "I wonder who's being obstinate now."

Her attitude shocked him. How could she think of Father as obstinate? Father, who wanted only the very best for his family? Fourteen-year-old Gerrit decided that sometime soon he would give Elsa a piece of his mind.

Rain was falling as the family stepped out into the dark street. Moisture seeped through Gerrit's coat. By the time they reached the basement entrance of the home where meeting was being held, he was wet through.

Yet his misery was forgotten as Brother Jan began to speak. At first he had much to say about sin, how it separates us from a holy God. Then Jan read these words from John 14: *I am the way, the truth, and the life.* Earnestly he explained that Jesus is the only way to be reconciled with God, because Jesus died to save us from sin. Oh, how Jesus suffered for our sakes! And if we are called to suffer for Christ's sake, Jan maintained, our sufferings are nothing compared to what Jesus went through.

As Gerrit listened, a picture of the North Sea entered his mind. He remembered what Father had said, that the sea was like God's "river of water of life"—a vast love that sought to claim his heart—the heart of Gerrit Lieven. We should not build dikes around our hearts, that minister back north had said. We should open up, and allow God's love to pour in…

CRASH! CRASH! The basement door splintered under heavy blows. Armed men exploded into the room, chains clanking and swords gleaming in the candlelight. Somewhere a woman screamed.

Heart pounding, Gerrit darted across the room and grabbed Elsa's hand. "Come! I know where the back entrance is."

Up a dark stairway they struggled, expecting any moment to feel rough hands upon them. But no, they broke free into the rain-washed air. Stealing along back alleys, they reached home.

This time, however, Father and Mother did not come.

Gerrit tried his best to comfort his sobbing sister. But how could he comfort someone else when his own heart was breaking? The day crept slowly by. There was nothing to do but wait…and wait.

Towards evening they came. Not Father and Mother, but two more bailiffs.

They spoke kindly enough. "Your parents are in prison. Surely you two don't want to stay here without them. Come with us; we know of a place where you can stay."

Too numb to resist, Gerrit and Elsa allowed themselves to be led through the twilit streets. Gerrit recognized right away the building to which they were taken.

It was the Catholic convent. Through the weariness of his mind passed a confused thought: *So we're to become Catholics now.*

The nuns brought them supper and then showed them to rooms for the night. When morning came, Gerrit realized that his utter weariness had put him to sleep. Even though Father and Mother were in prison. Even though, like so many other brethren, they would probably be executed in a week or so.

Gerrit and Elsa were served breakfast at a small table. No one else was around. Guardedly, Elsa whispered, "I overheard two nuns talking. You and I are to be baptized tomorrow."

Revulsion coursed through Gerrit. Baptized, by a Catholic priest? Baptized, without the confession of faith his parents so often spoke of? "Father wouldn't like that," he said, as vehemently as he could while whispering.

Elsa shook her head. "I know. But what can we do?"

"I won't let them," he whispered, still fiercely. "I'll run away. Somehow. Will you come too?"

So tired. Elsa looked so tired and vulnerable and sad. "We'll never see Father and Mother again," she said tearfully. "Where would we run to? Here, they'd at least be kind to us."

"You don't know that," he said savagely.

"I can feel it. And I'm ready for some kindness. Ready to stop being in danger. Please stay, Gerrit."

"No. I can't. I'm leaving. I'll find a way. And I'll come back for you someday, Elsa." Even as he uttered the words, Gerrit realized it was a very big promise to make.

In his room that day, Gerrit did some investigating. He knew the door would be locked that night. But what about the window? It slid open easily, and he smiled as he stuck his head outside. The distance to the ground was not that great. Nothing that knotted bedsheets couldn't handle.

At supper he made sure he ate well. No telling when he would next have a solid meal. "I'm leaving tonight," he told Elsa between bites. "But I'll be back someday."

"We don't know—about Father and Mother," she faltered. "Maybe they'll be allowed to go free. If they recant, you know…"

"They won't," he said, almost scoffing. "But listen, I'll stay around until—well, until I find out how things go for them. Then…it'll probably be the sea for me, Elsa. And after I've made some money, I'll come and get you out of this convent. Okay?"

Her only answer was a flood of tears.

His escape plan worked, almost too easily. If the convent grounds had guards, there were none that Gerrit saw. He slipped out between the massive gate and its post. Then he ran for a while, until his breath came in gasps.

It wasn't far to the harbor. Beneath an old dock he found a place where he could curl up and sleep. Day had not long broken before a dockworker offered him a penny if he helped load a ship. By noon, Gerrit was in possession of a loaf of bread.

It was a new, strange life—but not without its thrills. Harbor life helped him forget. He wanted to forget—everything. Well, everything except Elsa, because he had made a promise to her.

Sometimes, though, messages from meetings nudged at his mind. "Open your life to the Lord—confess your sins—be saved by Christ's mercy—live in obedience to Him." But Gerrit always pushed the messages away. Such things had not saved the lives of his parents.

He supposed they had been slain. Still, to make sure, he visited a church brother one day. Gilles acted so happy to see him, and eager to keep him, too. "You can work for me, be like a son to me," he offered.

Coldly, Gerrit asked, "So they're dead? Titelman killed my parents?"

Gilles looked startled. "I'm sorry. I thought you knew. Yes, they have gone to be with the Lord. Praise God, they remained steadfast."

Gerrit turned away. To him, such words were like vinegar on a wound. A feeling of having been abandoned by his parents washed over him. His gruff parting words to Gilles were, "I'll let you know if I need work."

Already the next day, a sailor tried to recruit him for a ship's crew. But Gerrit hesitated. He had heard about the Sea Beggars, how they sought to free the Netherlands from Spain. With them, he would have a purpose. Perhaps if he worked long enough on Antwerp's docks, he could somehow connect with a Sea Beggar ship.

He managed to scrape by, making enough money for food, finding places to sleep. Every now and then he made inquiries about the Sea Beggars. Here in this Catholic city he had to be careful who he asked, of course. But surely the pirates sometimes entered this harbor too.

Three weeks passed before he finally contacted the right man, who swiftly signed him on as boatswain for the *Hollander*. "Be on this dock tomorrow at noon, and I'll show up in a boat to take you off," the man instructed.

Using up his hard-earned money, Gerrit bought a second pair of trousers and a pair of boots. Then he stationed himself near the designated dock, hoping he did not look like a pirate in the making.

Soon a boat appeared, rowing against the current. Gerrit squinted until he felt sure it was the man who'd hired him. He slipped to the edge of the dock.

"Wait," said a voice, familiar, yet not familiar.

It was Gilles, hurrying toward him with a paper in his hand. "Praise God, I've found you. I've hunted for days. A letter came into my hands, and I promised to deliver it if I could. It's for you."

Accepting the paper, Gerrit dropped his eyes to the signature. There was no name—only "Your father and mother."

He stared at the handwriting. It swam before his eyes. Yes, it was Father's handwriting. "What—? How—?"

"They wrote letters while in prison. One for you and one for Elsa. She has hers already. Gerrit, your father would want you to come live with us. I'm sure of it."

A few words on the paper caught Gerrit's eye. There were loving admonitions and reminders of God's grace.

Gerrit dashed a hand across his eyes. He jerked a thumb toward the boat, now being tied up at the dock. "That man has hired me. Thanks anyway."

He turned, hoping no tear streaks remained for his new master to see.

chapter six

On the Garden Bench

Through the open window floated the children's happy chatter. Curious about their play, Gerrit pulled himself into a sitting position. He noticed with pleasure that his back barely hurt anymore.

"Let's play Sea Beggars!" That was Ghysbrecht's shrill voice.

Gerrit gripped the windowsill, hard. How would a boy and a girl play Sea Beggars? He watched them weaving back and forth on the lawn. Eventually he caught on that Tryntgen was pretending to be a Spanish ship, and Ghysbrecht a pirate. Now they grabbed sticks, clubbing and poking at each other.

Unbidden tears sprang to Gerrit's eyes. Such violence. And he was the cause of introducing it to this household. The children would hardly be thinking these things if their Sea Beggar uncle had not taken up residence in the spare bedroom.

A tap sounded on his door, and Elsa entered. "Why the tears, my brother?" she asked lightly.

"Regrets. Again. I am such a poor example to your children." He pointed to the window. "They're out there pretending to be in mortal combat, Dutch against Spanish."

"Oh, that's just play." Her voice stayed light as she straightened his sheets and fluffed the pillows.

"Play that would have horrified their nonresistant grandparents," Gerrit persisted. "Listen, I'm a lot better now. It's time I get out and make a living in the real world. Relieve these children of a bad example, too."

She came over and gazed through the window. "Just play," she repeated with a shrug. "And besides, nonresistant grandparents or not, they're Catholic. Nothing nonresistant about a Catholic."

He grimaced. "Bloodthirsty bunch, these Catholics. The Duke of Alba—why, he's beheading heretics at twice the rate Titelman used to manage."

"Alba is quite the governor," she agreed ruefully. "It's no wonder people call his Council of Troubles the 'Council of Blood' instead. But you know very well that not all Catholics are bloodthirsty. Jorg wouldn't hurt a flea."

Gerrit grinned. He couldn't help liking his sister's soft-hearted husband. "If it weren't for Jorg, I'd probably have still more regrets to deal with. Remember how, when I left Antwerp at fourteen years of age, I promised to come back and get you someday? Well, that 'someday' didn't happen for—what was it? Eight years?"

"Something like that. And when you came, I was happily married to Jorg. So, no, don't be regretful. Life at the convent had been quite bearable too. At least I didn't have to scrounge for a living." Elsa picked up a vase and removed a handful of dead-looking flowers. "If anything, I should be having regrets that I wasn't able to do more for you."

He waved a hand. "You've saved my life. What more could you do? But Elsa, we're being complacent. We both know this: we haven't lived up to what our parents would have desired."

"Must we talk about that?" A pained look crossed her face.

"Not if you don't want to. Could you please hand me my little leather bag? I still marvel that Jules made sure my possessions left the ship with me, half-dead though I was." Gerrit rummaged in the salt-smelling purse, seeking an inner compartment he had almost forgotten. Sure enough, a crackling greeted his fingers. The letter was still intact. When had he last even thought about it? Not for years.

Yet the sight of his father's handwriting brought fresh tears. It seemed to Gerrit that being an invalid made him extra susceptible to tears. They could be unhandy at times.

"Our dear son, we commend your life to the Lord. We pray that your few short years in our care have been enough to awaken in you a desire for the truth. Dear son, there is no peace on earth unless we have the truth. Jesus is that truth, and if we repent, believe, and obey, He is ours through the Holy Spirit..."

"Does your letter start in the same way as mine, Elsa?" Gerrit asked without looking up.

There was no answer. His sister had left the room.

He smiled wryly to himself. "Apparently I'll receive no help from her to improve my life. Whereas she wants to forget the past, to me it seems that is where I must look for help. To the past, with my parents' example of childlike dependence on Jesus."

Putting down the letter, Gerrit labored to his feet. "It's up to me to change things," he panted, shuffling toward the door.

Fortunately an outside entrance lay just a short way down the hall. Gripping his cane, he inched onto the grass. The ground was so treacherously uneven. What if he fell? Then he would only need more help.

But he made it to a bench not far from the children. They came running in delight. "I didn't know you can come outside, Uncle Gerrit!" Tryntgen beamed.

"I can if I try hard enough," he assured her. "Were you playing a pirate game?"

"Yes! I'm a Sea Beggar and she's Spanish," Ghysbrecht replied enthusiastically.

"Surely you could think up a nicer game than that," Gerrit reproached them. "Killing people is—terrible. We shouldn't even pretend to do it."

Bewilderment flooded his nephew's face. "But—you are a Sea Beggar. You did it all the time. Didn't you, Uncle Gerrit?"

"I regret it. Very much," he said without directly answering his question. "Come, don't you have a ball or something? If I could, I would like to play catch with you children. Three-cornered catch, maybe."

Tryntgen clapped her hands. "Let's! You can stay sitting on the bench, Uncle Gerrit. I'll stand by that tree, and Ghysbrecht, you go to the big flowerbed. Here's the ball!"

They played an awkward few rounds, with Gerrit fumbling more often than catching. Finally he wiped his brow and admitted, "I need to rest."

"You were sitting the whole time," Tryntgen pointed out innocently.

"I know. That goes to show how easily I tire. It'll take me a long time to regain the strength I used to have. Why, just these few minutes of playing ball have turned my legs and arms all quivery."

A movement in the garden caught his eye. Clad in a bright

bonnet, with a cheery apron tied over her dress, a girl stooped among the plants. "Who's that?" Gerrit asked.

"Oh, that's just Bettgen, the kitchen maid. She's nice, though," Tryntgen assured him.

"I see that," he said, nodding. He wished she would look up, perhaps even meet his eye.

"Mother says Bettgen was an orphan. That's why we took her in. Orphans don't have parents, you know," Tryntgen explained.

"Yes, I know. I'm an orphan too. So is your mother." The girl—Bettgen—had filled her basket and was heading for the back kitchen door. Not too much hope now anymore that she would glance in his direction.

Tryntgen looked grave. "Mother told me that Grandpa and Grandma Lieven were killed by an inquis—inquizzer. I think that's what she said."

"Inquisitor. Someone like the Duke of Alba. See? What I told you is true. Killing people is terrible." Gerrit wondered whether Bettgen's story was similar. The Netherlands must contain hundreds—or thousands—of orphans from Anabaptist parents.

As children will do, Tryntgen and Ghysbrecht suddenly lost interest in this somber topic and romped off elsewhere. Once Gerrit's legs had stopped quivering he drew himself upright and shuffled to the garden's edge. Ah. There was another bench, close to the path leading from the kitchen.

Next morning, quite early, Gerrit stationed himself on the garden bench. Soon footsteps tripped lightly toward him from behind—then hesitated, and stopped.

Donning his best smile, he turned his head. "Good morning. I suppose you've heard about your mistress's invalid brother. I'm Gerrit Lieven."

"And I—I'm Bettgen Vervest. Yes, I've heard of you, and I'm sorry about your injury." Her voice was low, modest.

"I brought it upon myself," he said brusquely. She was moving on beyond him now. Hoping to detain her a bit longer he asked, "How are the vegetables doing, Bettgen?"

"Very well, sir. It's a good summer."

"I can tell from the good meals brought my way." Now she was stooping over the bean plants, picking industriously. How could he find out about her background? Maybe if he spoke of his own...

"Has Elsa told you anything about her childhood?" he inquired.

She glanced his way, questions flickering in her eyes. "She told me that her—that your parents were Anabaptists and—and were slain because of it."

That was all she offered. She seemed so fearful. Why did she leave the garden before her basket was even half filled?

Pondering, Gerrit trudged back to the house. Perhaps the girl had experienced trouble in the past from dishonorable men. So if he wished to gain her friendship, he would need to be forthright and honest. Let her know exactly what his intentions were.

Startled at himself, Gerrit stopped in the middle of the path. What was happening anyway? Never before in his life had he entertained such thoughts about a maiden.

chapter seven

New Friendship

He decided to write her a letter. He knew he could have spoken to his sister, using her as his intermediary. But he wanted to do this his own way, and as privately as possible.

As for finding out about Bettgen's early life, no doubt Elsa could have filled him in. But that would rob him of the chance to hear things from Bettgen's lips.

"Dear Bettgen," he wrote, "I do not want to be bold or rude, but I humbly request your friendship so that we can learn to know each other better. If God so leads, we might then consider being joined in marriage. Yours truly, Gerrit Lieven." At the bottom he added, "For reply, you may slip a letter under my door."

He reread his words. "If God so leads." What had made him write that? When had he ever taken God's leading into consideration? Was he trying to give Bettgen the impression he was a God-fearing man?

Deep in his heart, Gerrit knew one thing: he would like to be a

God-fearing man. But how to become one was beyond him.

Taking a walk toward the back of the house, Gerrit rejoiced to find the kitchen empty. He placed the letter—with Bettgen's name prominently displayed—on a shelf inside the door. Then he fled to his room.

How soon could he expect a reply? Not that day, he hoped. If her answer came too soon it would certainly be a no.

The next day and the next, he nearly wore a hole into the floor near the door, watching for the arrival of a letter. Much to his chagrin, it was Elsa who finally brought him one.

"You tried to pull it off behind my back!" she accused with a big smile as she handed him the letter. "But Bettgen spoiled things for you by taking me into her confidence. You see, she is more than a kitchen maid to me. Almost a sister."

His face burned. "If I'd known that, I might have—might have asked you to be the go-between."

"That's okay. A man needs to do things on his own. Women tend to ask for advice. That's what Bettgen did, and Gerrit, I'm afraid my advice was rather biased."

"So you told her she'd better have nothing to do with this pirate."

"I certainly did not! I spoke highly of you. Told her you're more of a deep thinker than I am."

He stared at the letter. Did he dare to open it?

"I'll leave you alone now." His sister made a hasty exit.

He smoothed out the page. "Dear sir," she began, and he thought, *Why so formal?*

"I feel I do not know you at all, yet your sister has been very good to me. If you so wish, we might meet to visit. Yours respectfully, Bettgen."

"If you so wish." Did she doubt it? Had she no idea how his heart desired a visit with her?

She had said yes. Elation made Gerrit feel as if he could get up and walk a mile without effort. Reality, of course, told him otherwise.

One thought bothered him. In her letter Bettgen emphasized that Elsa had been so good to her. Was Bettgen perhaps accepting his friendship only out of duty, because she did not want to disappoint her employer? If that was the case, then…then their relationship was not off to a good start.

Well, the only way to untangle these mysteries was learning to know one another. Through Elsa this time, Gerrit arranged to meet Bettgen at the garden bench, which was in full view of the house. Skulking in corners would not do. He wanted Bettgen's confidence.

Their first visit was on a Sunday afternoon. He wondered whether she felt as awkward as he did. Their conversation was stiff, and it stayed with everyday subjects such as the garden's progress and the children's doings. None of Gerrit's questions about Bettgen were answered; he guessed if she'd had questions about him, none of those had been answered either.

Oh well, he had plenty of time. Bettgen, on the other hand, had work to do and could not spend much time visiting on weekdays. They agreed that an hour on Wednesday evenings was all they could spend together other than Sunday afternoons.

During their next visit, Gerrit shared some memories of life on the farm in Groningen. "Maybe Elsa has spoken to you about the old plowhorse named Rippert. She was pretty sad to leave him."

"I believe she has mentioned Rippert," Bettgen said with a nod. "And wasn't there a pig with a name as well?"

He chuckled. "Elsa called the pig Amy, I think." Glancing toward the garden, he queried, "Does Elsa work in this garden at all?"

"If she does, I haven't seen her at it," came the reply.

"Elsa must have changed a lot. She used to enjoy gardening, digging in the dirt, things like that. Oh well, I guess I've changed a lot too." He glanced at her. "I wouldn't blame you for feeling uncomfortable in the company of a pirate. Um—I would like to say I'm a former pirate."

"That's how I prefer to think about it too," she said simply.

"Losing my parents set me adrift. The Sea Beggars gave me a—a sense of belonging to something, I guess. Of course I see now that I could have found a better place to belong. But when you're fourteen…" His let his voice trail off.

Sympathetically she said, "I think I have some idea. I was thirteen when my parents died."

"Died? They weren't—slain?"

She shook her head. "They took ill and died in prison. Father first, then Mother. Prison life isn't very healthy."

"True. My parents weren't in prison long enough to get sick." He paused. "Were you ever—did you ever struggle with the feeling that your parents abandoned you because of their faith?"

"Yes, in a way. I kept asking myself how they could consider their faith more important than their children."

They fell silent. Their relationship was almost too new to bare their hearts like this.

After a minute Bettgen continued, "When my parents were gone, the bailiffs were hard on us children. My oldest brother was eighteen and had actually joined the Mennonites already. But the authorities persuaded him to return to the Catholics. With my next brother, Hansken, it was a different story. He was only fifteen, yet when they tried to coerce him into Catholicism, he refused. Simply refused. He eventually escaped from the Gravensteen prison and went to live on his own. Father and Mother would have been happy with his choice, I suppose; he received baptism from the Mennonites. For me it was very confusing. Which brother should I take as an example?"

A lump came into Gerrit's throat as he nodded slowly. What a challenge for a girl of thirteen!

"I was brought to trial," she went on. "They forced me to give information about my parents and some other church members."

Gerrit growled, "That's no way to treat a young girl."

"I guess I didn't have Hansken's strength of character. I just meekly submitted, and allowed the Catholics to baptize me," she confessed. "That way I was allowed to leave the Gravensteen. I hated it there."

"No doubt." Gerrit realized his hands had doubled into fists. To think what Bettgen had gone through!

"I will always be grateful to your sister for taking me in as a kitchen maid," Bettgen said. "I have been happy here. Though sometimes..." She hesitated. "Sometimes I wonder what my parents would think. To them, death was better than giving up their faith. Now I, and all my seven brothers and sisters except Hansken, are Catholic."

Gerrit mused, "It makes you wonder—was it worth it? Yes, our parents remained steadfast, but what good did it do if the children were unable to receive the faith because they lost their parents' support?"

Bettgen looked startled. "I would not want to question what my parents did. At least Hansken stood firm."

"He was fifteen, you said. Hmmm. Pretty young for such a strong faith. Where is he now?"

"He got married and became a minister, then was soon slain. His wife… I think she got married again and is now living in the Danzig area. She sometimes writes to me."

"I see. Interesting, that she hasn't forgotten you."

"In a way I like it too. Yet it keeps my conscience disturbed. I'm not allowed to forget the hopes my parents had for me. Though I am quite settled now in the Catholic Church," she added defensively.

He said nothing. He wondered if she knew that he was not a Catholic.

Part Two
Bettgen

chapter eight

Warning from Irema

Bettgen slid from the garden bench. "I must go, or else I'll get a scolding from Irema." It was Wednesday evening, and once again her hour with Gerrit had seemed much too short.

"Who is Irema?" he asked curiously.

Bettgen was startled. "Have I never told you? She's the cook. You've eaten many a meal prepared by Irema."

"Well, I like her cooking, but I don't like it that she scolds you," Gerrit said with a grimace.

Bettgen stood looking down at this man whom she was learning to love. Though she knew he still dealt daily with pain, he appeared much better these days. Color was returning to his face. "Irema is such an orderly, punctual person," Bettgen explained. "If things are not on time she becomes gruff. She expects my help tonight for some of tomorrow's dinner preparations, and I must not be late."

Still Gerrit's face was grim. "She shouldn't be allowed to treat you like that. Does Elsa know?"

Bettgen let out a peal of laughter. "Please don't worry about Irema, Gerrit! Beneath all the gruffness she has a soft heart. I'm sure of it."

"Then I hope her heart is soft tonight," he called after her as she tripped lightly toward the house.

Soft-hearted cook or not, Bettgen's own heart sang within her. What a pleasure, to have someone like Gerrit care so much for her! Never before had she enjoyed a man's friendship.

I'm as happy as a very young girl, Bettgen thought. *Yet here I am at the ripe old age of twenty-five. Oh well, Gerrit is older still. We make a good pair.* She pushed open the kitchen door.

Hands on hips, Irema turned from the bubbling pot on the hearth. Disheveled gray hair wreathed her stern face. "You are late. Hard telling when we'll get to bed, with all the preparations we must do."

Trying to sound contrite, Bettgen replied, "I'm sorry. Where shall I start?"

Ignoring her question, Irema snarled, "You're not really sorry. I can see you've fallen head over heels for that no-good pirate. Let me tell you, Bettgen, you should be extremely wary of him. Here. Peel these potatoes."

The cook's unpleasant words sent a chill into Bettgen's heart. "No-good pirate…you should be extremely wary." Why did Irema feel thus about Gerrit?

While chopping vegetables for the stew, Irema ranted on. "Take it from me. I have experience. You shouldn't trust that man. I once trusted a man—but look where I am now."

Feeling sorry for the bitter old woman, Bettgen said hesitantly, "I—I guess I don't know what happened to you."

"He deserted me. I have a husband, but I don't know where he is. That's why I tell young people they'd be better off not marrying. Men can't be trusted." Irema's rancor seemed to fill the kitchen.

When Bettgen said nothing, Irema continued, "This Gerrit is a Sea Beggar, is he not?"

"He was. He is not going back." Bettgen forced her voice to be firm.

"That's what he says," snorted Irema. "I'm surprised Jorg will have anything to do with Gerrit. Those Sea Beggars have done a lot of damage to the Netherlands' economy. Trade is disrupted because of these pirate ships roaming the coast. I'm pretty sure Jorg's business has also suffered from the Sea Beggars' activities."

Bettgen's fingers went numb. To think that only a few minutes ago, she had felt so light-hearted and blissful as she left Gerrit's side. Now Irema's tirade was poisoning her happiness. "I don't know very much about these things," Bettgen said unsteadily. "But I doubt that Gerrit would intentionally do harm to the Netherlands."

"Ha! You doubt it? I'll say it again—you'd better ask some questions and find out what really is in this man's heart," Irema insisted.

That night in her narrow attic bed, Bettgen tossed and turned. Was Irema right? Should she be wary? Could Gerrit really not be trusted?

Finally Bettgen decided she would tell Elsa about the conversation with Irema. After that she slept.

Opportunities to chat with her employer were not easy to come by. But several days later, Bettgen was delighted to find Elsa sitting on the garden bench. Picking beans from a row nearby, Bettgen began, "Irema doesn't like Gerrit. She warned me that I shouldn't trust him."

Elsa's eyebrows rose. "Irema is a sad, bitter woman. Did she tell you what happened with her marriage?"

"A little. It must have been hard."

"The whole affair turned her against men in general. So what slander has she been directing at my brother?"

"Oh, she says she's surprised Jorg can be so kind to a pirate who was hurting the Netherlands' economy by disrupting trade. Do you think Gerrit would intentionally do anything against our country?" Bettgen asked.

"No, I don't," Elsa replied with a smile. "Listen, Bettgen, I suggest you talk with Gerrit about these things. I believe he'll be open with you. Try to discover what his motives were in helping the Sea Beggars."

Bettgen recalled, "Another time, he made it sound as though joining them was sort of a—a reaction to being orphaned."

"Still, something must have kept him loyal all these years. Could be he really likes the Prince of Orange. Ask him," Elsa urged.

So after studying how to word it, Bettgen asked this question during her next visit with Gerrit. "What do you think of William, Prince of Orange?"

Instantly a glow lit his eyes. "He's the Netherlands' only hope!"

Taken aback by his enthusiasm, she asked, "What do you mean by that?"

Apologetically he said, "I must remember that not everyone is so eager to see our provinces freed from King Philip of Spain. But surely you agree that Philip is a selfish king who cares only for the good of Spain?"

"I've heard a few things in that line," she admitted. "Would you say most of the Dutch people wish to be free from Spain's rule—

not just the Calvinist people, but also the Catholics?"

"Well, I know of many Catholics who feel like I do. The Duke of Alba, our governor, is a heartless man. Surely you do not agree with the way he is killing heretics?"

She shook her head. "No. No. He is terrible. And you think William has the power to conquer Alba?"

"I hope so. It's true that William's armies met with defeat last year when he attempted to fight the Spanish. But it was partly the fault of the Dutch people. They did not rise up and help William the way they should have."

"Tell me what you know about William," she encouraged.

He sat up straighter. "William is a fair-minded man. His vision for the Netherlands is religious freedom—meaning that Catholics and Calvinists should be allowed to exist side by side. That's why he was greatly disappointed by the 'breaking of the images' riots of 1566."

"Oh. So he was disappointed," breathed Bettgen. "I'd been told William was the leader of the riots."

"Indeed, no! William did everything he could to stop them!" Gerrit flared.

"That was a terrible time," Bettgen recalled with a shudder. "The riots were at their worst here in Antwerp. Calvinists breaking into Catholic churches, spoiling everything, tearing down images of the saints, breaking beautiful stained-glass windows..."

"Hundreds of churches had their interiors destroyed," Gerrit agreed. "And William was dismayed. He knew the whole thing had done far more harm than good. Now a huge, implacable barrier had arisen between Catholics and Calvinists. And King Philip had all the more reason to punish Calvinists. He did it with a vengeance. By 1567 he sent the cruel, heartless Alba to be governor. Do you see now why I feel the Dutch people brought it on themselves?"

"Yes, I do. And I'm glad I know now that William had no part in the riots."

"The trouble is, people did not understand William's good intentions. He was mistrusted by many—particularly the Duke of Alba. William realized he would have to flee from the Netherlands. He went back to his old home, the German estate of Dillenburg, where his mother was still living. He was safe there, at least for the time being."

Gerrit sat back, crossing his hands behind his head. "But the Duke of Alba tried to get him. In January of 1568 Alba issued a command for William to appear before his 'Council of Troubles.' William knew better than to obey. Several other noblemen had been tried by the Council, and they were hanged. William stayed home in Dillenburg.

"That didn't keep Alba from passing judgment on Prince William. All the lands William owned in the Netherlands were taken from him. Worst of all, William's son was sent off to Spain. Father and son haven't seen each other since."

"So cruel," Bettgen murmured.

"In April of 1968," Gerrit continued, "a group of Dutchmen traveled to Dillenburg and told William the Netherlands is ready to rise up and throw off Spain's yoke. They asked William to be their leader, and he agreed. He sold everything he owned in order to raise money to hire an army. Even before William marched to the Netherlands, his brother Lodewyk had done battle with the Spanish at Heiligerlee, in the province of Groningen. Maybe you remember that."

"I do." She nodded. "Lodewyk defeated the Spanish there, didn't he?"

"Yes. The one sad thing was that another brother of William's, Adolf, lost his life in that battle. But still, Heiligerlee served as a great encouragement for William. With high hopes he marched to Brabant at the head of his hired army."

"I remember that. I was afraid, because the fighting was coming close to Antwerp," Bettgen admitted.

"The battle was a disaster. In fact, there was no battle. For one thing, like I said, the Dutch people did not make good on their promise to help William. They were too scared of Alba. And the other thing was that the crafty Alba knew William's hired soldiers would fight only as long as they were paid. When William's money ran out, they deserted him. Alba won without a fight. Defeated and poverty-stricken, William fled to France. As far as I know he's still there."

"Yet you still think William of Orange is the Netherlands' only hope?" she probed.

"I think so, yes. But only if the people support him."

An involuntary shiver went through Bettgen. She had learned a few things, not only about William of Orange, but about Gerrit too. As far as she could tell, there was nothing about which she ought to be "extremely wary."

· Open the Dikes ·

chapter nine

Unbaptized

It was Sunday evening, and Bettgen Vervest could not sleep. She had sensed, during their afternoon visit, that something was bothering Gerrit.

What could it be? Was he having second thoughts? Did he wish he had not become entangled with his sister's kitchen maid? Was he starting to pine for the sea again, now that his strength was returning?

"I cannot do without you, Gerrit," Bettgen sobbed into the pillow. "Do you not see how much I love you and need you? Can you break my heart by saying good-bye?"

The weeks had flown by so fast. Now it was spring of 1570. Bettgen wondered why Gerrit did not ask her to marry him. Gradually a cloud of foreboding had shadowed her horizon. Today, when he had seemed so preoccupied and even withdrawn, the cloud mushroomed into a looming disaster.

How Bettgen dreaded facing Irema that Monday morning!

The cook was so sharp. She would almost certainly notice that something was on her mind.

Yet not facing her would be even worse, since it would bring down a string of scathing words upon her head. So Bettgen trudged down the narrow stairway and entered the steamy kitchen.

"Here you come! The porridge is already scorched because you were not here to stir it," snapped Irema.

Lurching to the fireplace, Bettgen grabbed the big wooden spoon and stirred vigorously. With a sinking feeling she noticed how the spoon stuck to the bottom of the pot. What would Gerrit think if his porridge tasted burnt this morning?

"Your head is too full of that pirate," grumbled Irema. "I'm still hoping you come to your senses someday soon and show him to the door. Why, he's an invalid! How could he expect to support a family?"

At first Bettgen felt like screaming. But suddenly a light went on in her head. That was it. Without knowing what she'd done, Irema had given her an inkling of what was troubling Gerrit.

In her most dignified voice Bettgen replied to the cook, "I have reason to believe he is working on the question of how he will support me."

Irema ranted on, but Bettgen was deaf to her remarks. Her mind teemed with solutions to Gerrit's dilemma. If he was worried about making a living, surely he could find an easy job with a weaver, or a tailor. Or what about Jorg's large merchandising enterprise? Surely not all the positions would entail hard physical labor.

By evening she'd persuaded herself that Gerrit might be grateful if she'd broach the subject. Taking a seat near him in the drawing room, she thought she sensed his moodiness. What should she say, and how?

He let out a heavy sigh and began, "I feel I did you an injustice in asking for your friendship."

Her heart plummeted. "Why do you say that?"

Agitated fingers combed his blonde hair. "Because how can we go on from here? I'm little more than a cripple. I would like to ask you to marry me, but how could I support a wife?"

Bettgen smiled—a wide, happy smile. "Please do, Gerrit. Please ask me to marry you."

Slowly a smile spread across his face too. "All right. Bettgen, will you marry me?"

"Yes," she replied simply. "And as for supporting me, surely there are jobs available for one who is not quite strong."

He spread his hand. "I've looked around some, and had no success."

"I sensed something was bothering you," she told him.

"Was it that obvious? Anyway, I feel unworthy that you trust me enough to say yes."

Again their hour was not long enough, because now they had many plans to make. Wedding plans, housing plans, work plans. By the time Bettgen had put forth all her suggestions, Gerrit was able to take a positive view once more.

Even after they had parted, Bettgen's busy mind kept churning out ideas. Maybe she should take matters into her own hands. The very next day she managed to catch her employer when no one else was around. By way of a rather obvious hint, she began, "Gerrit has been trying to find work."

Elsa fell for the bait immediately. "I'm glad to hear he feels well enough. I must say something to Jorg. Surely the company would have an opening for a man like Gerrit."

"I thought maybe you could help," Bettgen admitted with a

broad smile.

Things happened fast. By Sunday Gerrit reported that Jorg had hired him as an accountant. Bettgen made sure he didn't suspect that she was behind this.

"And Jorg even had a suggestion for a home!" Gerrit added triumphantly.

"Is that so! Where?"

"Right here. You know that big carriage house near the gate? Apparently they are using less than half the space. Jorg thinks part of it could be renovated into a small home." Gerrit straightened his shoulders. "We would be renting. I told him it's time I stopped accepting charity and started paying my own way."

Bettgen could not help feeling proud of him. Though still gaunt and weak, he hated being a burden to anyone. "Tomorrow," she said merrily, "I will tell Irema that we are engaged."

He grinned. "She will hardly jump for joy."

"I really don't care what her reaction will be," responded Bettgen, and they laughed together.

In spite of those brave words, Bettgen's knees quivered the next morning in the kitchen. If only she could keep the quiver out of her voice! "I wanted to tell you, Irema—Gerrit and I are getting married this summer."

"And where will you find a priest to perform such a marriage?" the cook shot back.

"Why, we would ask Father Hoogeveen, of course," Bettgen replied pleasantly.

"Try it. He will ask you questions that you'll find hard to answer. Such as whether Gerrit is a Catholic." A sneer laced Irema's voice.

Bettgen felt as if she had been slapped in the face. "Of course Gerrit is a Catholic. I wouldn't dream of marrying someone who isn't."

"Have you ever seen him at Mass?" Irema's eyes narrowed. "Have you ever heard of a Catholic Sea Beggar?"

"You can't treat me like this!" Bettgen ran sobbing from the kitchen.

She fled up the back stairway to her own room. Her world seemed to lie in a thousand splintered shards at her feet. No, she had never seen Gerrit at Mass, but she'd attributed that to his illness. It was the cook's final words that quivered like a poison barb in her heart. Sea Beggars were Calvinists. Why had the thought never occurred to her? How could she have kept company with a Calvinist all these months?

She shuddered. Why had she and Gerrit never discussed these things?

Occasionally they had talked about God. Gerrit believed in Him; of that, Bettgen felt certain. After all, he had grown up in a Mennonite home. Just like her.

But she'd never heard him mention baptism. Could it be that he wasn't baptized at all? The thought filled her with horror.

For the moment, Bettgen felt she never wanted to see Gerrit again. After a while, though, the agitation in her heart died down.

She needed to talk to Elsa. Or, wait. Maybe she needed to go straight to Gerrit.

Drying her eyes, she scrambled from her part of the loft through a trapdoor into the main house's second story. Down the wide central staircase she crept. She peeked first into the drawing room, then into the library.

Ah, there was Elsa. Hands wrapped nervously in her apron, Bettgen went to her and whispered, "Irema was misusing me."

Elsa's head jerked up. "What's going on?"

"Please—if you could take me to Gerrit, I'd like to speak with him before I tell you." Bettgen's throat felt dry.

Leaping up, Elsa led her to Gerrit's room and knocked on the door. "Bettgen would like to speak with you."

"Let her come in," came his voice through the door.

Bettgen stepped over the threshold. Sitting near the fireplace, Gerrit looked pale and thin.

Elsa closed the door quietly. The two of them were alone. Bettgen cleared her throat. "There's something I need to know. You are a Catholic, are you not?"

His eyes fastened steadily on her face. "No, I am not. I thought you knew that."

The room spun around her. She reached out, gripping the door jamb. "No one told me. Gerrit, I can't marry someone who isn't Catholic."

"I see." His voice was measured, quiet. The room lay in silence for what seemed a long time. Then he said, almost lightly, "I believe I could become a Catholic. It's not that I haven't considered it."

"Oh, would you? But—surely you've been baptized before this?" She was almost pleading.

"No. You know how it is. I was born in a Mennonite home. Mennonites believe you must be accountable before you can be baptized. But you know what happened. I never got that far."

Her grip tightened on the door jamb. She had been keeping company with an unbaptized man!

He must have seen the horror in her face. "You Catholics believe that outward ceremonies save us. Right? Baptism saves. Mass saves. Prayers to the saints save. So now you are thinking that I am an unsaved man."

What could she say? He was putting her thoughts into words.

"Think back to your youth, Bettgen. Remember those meetings

you attended with your parents. I remember some of the things I heard when I was young. They have stuck with me. I cannot forget the idea that it takes more than outward ceremonies to save a person." Reaching for a blanket, he draped it over his knees.

Her blood ran cold. "Are you saying you'd rather be a Mennonite?"

"I guess not! That would be jumping from the frying pan into the fire," he snorted. "No, Bettgen, I'm willing to become a Catholic. Just take me to your friar, or whatever you call him."

She let out a long, trembling breath. She knew his light-hearted speech should worry her. But she did not want to think about that. She only wanted to get married—to a Catholic.

chapter ten

A Rite for Gerrit

"No."

In shock and disbelief, Bettgen stared at Gerrit as she absorbed his answer to her question. "But why not?" she protested. "Why wouldn't you want me there when you get baptized?"

His gaze was stony. "Because it's going to be embarrassing. Think about it, Bettgen. Father Hoogeveen is used to baptizing babies. Performing upon a grown man rites that are intended for babies…like I said, it's going to be embarrassing. For Father Hoogeveen, for me—and for whoever might be watching. So I decided there will be no watchers."

Bettgen clasped and unclasped her hands. Up to now, Gerrit had catered to her every wish. His greatest delight had seemed to be in doing things that made her happy. Was this cold, obstinate-looking man the same Gerrit she had known in the past months? How could he start turning against her now, when they were planning to get married?

Gerrit's voice grated on. "This baptism will be nothing like the ones you and I used to witness when we were young and with the Mennonites. I remember those times. The brethren used to be filled with—with holy thankfulness. Or something like that. The baptism itself was not even the main focus. The faith they confessed—that was the focus. My baptism will be nothing but an empty rite performed on a man whose heart is not in it."

He seemed almost to enjoy rubbing it in. His words were like weapons, and Bettgen felt like one big bleeding wound. She whispered, "I'm sorry. I shouldn't have pushed you into this."

He waved dismissively. "You didn't. Not really. I wouldn't have let you push me if I didn't want to do it. We know that the only way we can get married is if we're both Catholic. We also know…" Here the snarl crept back into his voice. "That it's quite possible to become a Catholic in name only, without involving the heart at all. Because Catholics believe that the performing of rites can magically save you."

She breathed heavily. Sobs threatened. "Gerrit, it hurts me so much that you feel this way. If only I could somehow help you, so that your heart could—could be in it…"

Getting to his feet, he paced back and forth near the garden bench. "There's no way, Bettgen. I decided I'd be honest with you. I won't pretend. That's why I'm being so blunt. Be grateful that I want to be honest, Bettgen."

Swallowing a sob, she gasped, "I'll try. I am glad for your honesty, Gerrit…but sometimes honesty hurts."

"Sorry," he said brusquely. "We're in this together. Sooner or later you'll find out what kind of man I am. It's not all pretty. But I intend to be honest with you."

"I'm glad," she said again.

Then it was Monday morning. Bettgen dreaded meeting the cook. True, Elsa had promised to give Irema a talking-to about how she should use her kitchen maid. But how much would that help? A talking-to would not bring an overnight change in the cook's crusty personality.

It seemed Irema always managed to discover Bettgen's most painful spots, which she then proceeded to attack. This morning, Irema kept her voice low. But that did not remove the acid edge. "I hear you've persuaded your man to get baptized."

Hastily, Bettgen turned her back and stirred the porridge. "He has decided he wants to be Catholic," she said stiffly. What she actually wanted to do was scream at Irema, asking how she found out these things.

Irema plunked down the basket of eggs and began breaking them into the pan. "Take it from me: if he's doing it only to please you, it won't last. He'll turn against you. Men always turn against women who try to manipulate them. They may seem compliant for a while, but eventually they refuse to take it anymore. Let me tell you, if you want your man, don't push him."

Wonderingly, Bettgen realized that Irema's voice was almost kind. Could it be that she truly cared for her kitchen maid and wished, in her own gruff way, to help? "Well, I—thanks for your advice," she stammered.

Opening the door, Irema peered down the alley. "Pavel! Where are you? Breakfast is ready to go."

Relieved at the interruption, Bettgen helped load food onto the trolley. Pavel would wheel it to the great dining room and set the steaming dishes on the table, where they would be enjoyed by Elsa's family. And by Gerrit. At least she hoped he could enjoy his breakfast this morning, with the baptism looming this afternoon.

Later that day, Bettgen had an opportunity to talk with Elsa in the garden. "Are you surprised that I didn't go to Gerrit's baptism?" she asked her employer.

Elsa thought for a moment before replying. "Not really. Gerrit is a private kind of person—more so than most men, I think. He'll want this to be between him and Father Hoogeveen."

Although Bettgen felt she could have told her otherwise, she decided not to comment. Instead she said, "Cook thinks he's doing it only for my sake, and therefore it will have no value."

Elsa's eyes narrowed. "Cook being hard on you again?"

"Sort of. She wasn't quite so loud this time."

"If she weren't such a good cook, we'd fire her," Elsa declared. "I don't know where she thinks she gets her authority to use you like this."

Bettgen pulled a few more onions. "But really—do you think it will work like Cook says? I mean, that the baptism has no value if—if his heart is not in it?"

"Ah, Bettgen, don't you fret," Elsa said lightly. "Things will work out. You two love each other, and that's what counts."

"I hope so," breathed Bettgen.

Elsa gave her a queer look. "You hope you love each other?"

"No, no. We do! I just hope it's the love that counts." Bettgen laughed shrilly.

"Have you discussed wedding plans?" Elsa went on.

"A little. But we know it can't be anything grand. We have no money."

Elsa's hands went to her hips. "If my brother is marrying my favorite kitchen maid, Jorg and I want to give them a wedding worth remembering."

"Oh—you are too kind," Bettgen faltered.

"Not so. Bettgen, I must admit I've been dreaming about your wedding. I mean, dreaming in a practical way, such as who would be the groomsman and bridesmaids, and what food we'd serve for the feast. I only hope you'll allow me to live my dreams!"

"If you really mean it…" Bettgen knew her eyes must be shining. Never had she dared to hope that a lowly kitchen maid could aspire to a real wedding! The two women were soon lost in their plans.

As Wednesday evening approached, however, trepidation gnawed at Bettgen's dreams. What if Gerrit said no again?

Surely he would not. Surely he would see how much she had set her heart on having a fine wedding. Gerrit was not really a hard-hearted man, was he?

In a rush of words she poured out their plans to him. Watching his face, her exhilaration wavered. He did not look impressed.

Even before she stopped talking, he was shaking his head. "I'm not interested in an elaborate wedding."

"Oh," she said, wondering how he could so callously disappoint her. "A wedding at the cathedral would make it seem more—well, more real, I guess."

His head was still shaking. "I don't agree. All we need for a real wedding is a priest to pronounce the blessing on our marriage. That can take place anywhere. Here in the garden, if you like. I'm already far more beholden to my sister than I would prefer. I will not let her bestow a grand wedding on top of her mountain of benevolence."

Bettgen tried one more tactic. "Elsa will be very disappointed."

"Then let her be. She will not rule over our lives, regardless how obligated we are to her and Jorg. And Bettgen, there's another reason why we don't want a grand wedding. Surely you understand what that reason is."

She stared sullenly at her hands. He was imposing his will on her, saying "we" don't want—as though he expected her to obey.

Unaware of her rebellious thoughts, he went on, "I have memories from my youth—and I'm sure you do too—of couples standing up at the end of a meeting and being joined in marriage by the minister. Were those real weddings? I believe they were."

"When you talk so wistfully about those days, I start thinking we really should pursue the thought of going back to our roots," she said in a low voice.

He let out a coarse laugh. "The Mennonites have no future, Bettgen. I've said it before, but that fact is more real than ever to me now. From the building where I work, I have a view of the Steen castle. Twice, now, I have seen ugly black clouds of smoke rise from the castle courtyard. Jorg says it happens at least once a month."

"Burning people at the stake," she whispered, her mouth dry.

"Yes. Burning is usually the fate of the men. The women get strangled, or drowned in the Scheldt River. The Duke of Alba is absolutely determined to rid the Netherlands of heretics."

She shuddered. "How can he live with himself? It's horrible."

"I agree. But what can we do? The Prince of Orange seems to have given up the cause of Dutch freedom. He still hides in France. Oh, that he could triumph over the Spanish, and that the orange, white, and blue flag of William would fly over every town in the Netherlands! But someone told me that the Duke of Alba has sneeringly said, 'William of Orange is a dead man.'"

The intensity of his emotions shook Bettgen. Apparently the struggle against the Spanish was still very real in his mind. No wonder that he found Catholicism distasteful! The Prince of

Orange, she knew, had forsaken the Catholic Church.

She had wanted to ask Gerrit tonight how the baptism had gone, but now she hardly dared.

He looked up suddenly. "What's this about the priest putting salt in the mouth of someone who gets baptized?"

She felt the heat rising to her face. "So they did that to you too. They do it to babies. It's—well, Jesus said His followers are the salt of the earth. That salt on the tongue, well, it's supposed to ensure that the person becomes...er..." She found her voice trailing off. The whole thing did seem rather ridiculous.

"It must be horrible for babies! I spat it out right away." Gerrit drew a hand across his mouth, as though still trying to get rid of the taste. "So I gather it's another sacrament, designed to bring about by outward ceremony what God says must spring from the heart."

She looked at him. "You seem to know a lot about God's will."

"Memories," he said with a grimace. "I wish I could just throw my memories into the Scheldt River and watch them float out to the North Sea, never to be seen again."

chapter eleven

Unexpected Freight

Bettgen stared disconsolately out the carriage house window. A raw March wind drove gray sheets of rain across the yard and garden. With all the rain that had fallen lately, it would be days before she could start planting. That was the only thing she could look forward to this spring: getting down on her knees and dropping seeds into the soil.

Bettgen sighed. She missed her kitchen duties. Of course she had a tiny kitchen of her own now, here in the carriage house, and she did enjoy cooking for Gerrit. But it was not like the big, sumptuous meals she used to help with.

"Well, it's my own fault that I can't work in the kitchen anymore," she reminded herself. "I complained once too often about Irema. Elsa was kind about it, but she told me she and Jorg had decided one of us would have to go. And since they really couldn't do without Irema, I was the one who got fired."

Yes, Elsa had been very kind, back in December when the

decision was made. She'd even worded it as though they were allowing Bettgen the privilege of being released from duties in the big house, since she now had work of her own to occupy her. Then, upon seeing Bettgen's disappointment, she had offered that there would be work for her in the garden once spring came.

Bettgen sighed again. Would spring ever come? Was life meant to be one big disappointment?

Oh, she and Gerrit had shared many happy newlywed hours last summer and fall. And he was still nice to her. Mostly, anyway. Yet sometimes she felt a chill creeping into their relationship, like the sly damp breezes that seeped through cracks into their makeshift dwelling here in the carriage house.

Also, looming large in their life was a nagging question. Why was there no promise of children? They had been married for eight months now. Though neither of them said much about it, she knew it lay on Gerrit's mind.

Ah, there he was now, coming home from work. She reveled in the way he walked these days: head erect, a spring in his steps. So unlike the sick man she had first learned to know. Many, many times she sent prayers of thanks to the Virgin for restoring her husband's health. Was he thankful too? Surely, but to whom he gave thanks remained a question.

Opening the door, he reached up and slipped over his head the strap of his leather purse. Coins clinked as he thudded it onto the table.

Just then his eyes slid to the window. "Oh, I see Jorg on the driveway. I just remembered something I was going to tell him." With that he disappeared out the door again.

Bettgen pulled the purse's drawstring. Slowly she fingered each coin. A month's pay. Fourteen guilders. More than adequate for rent and food and clothes.

Suddenly curious, she crossed the room to Gerrit's writing desk and opened his ledger, where he carefully recorded household accounts. Last month, and the month before, and the month before that, he had recorded only ten guilders. Why fourteen this month? Had he been getting fourteen every month, yet recording only ten?

Deciding not to say anything about it, she reclosed the drawstring.

A damp draft blew inside with him when he returned. "Such a wet day! I'll need a change of clothes, Bettgen."

Later, as they ate supper, he explained why he had gone out to speak with Jorg. "We've ordered some iron parts from Amsterdam, and they're coming on a ship tomorrow. I just found out this afternoon that the ship will also be carrying several tons of wool, bound for England. The wool isn't on order, though, so I wanted to ask Jorg why we don't unload it here, as we're going to need wool in a couple of weeks anyway."

She smiled at him. "You must be one of Jorg's right-hand men, if you help him make decisions like that."

"He does take me into his confidence quite a bit," he replied with a shrug.

In a rare burst of tenderness she told him, "I'm so glad you like your work." The look that passed over his face left her puzzled; it was almost as though he'd wanted to snort, "So you think!"

It was just another of many puzzling moments she had accosted in their marriage. Were all men as hard to understand as Gerrit? Had he not said, during their courtship, that he wished to be open and honest with her? Yet why did she so often sense something secretive about him?

The next morning she checked his ledger again. Under the date, March 6, he had written "10 guilders."

Desperately she scanned the page. The other four did not show up anywhere. What was Gerrit doing with those extra four guilders every month?

The question haunted her. What could he be doing that needed to stay hidden from his wife? Was he involved in criminal activities? Strong drink? Smuggling?

He certainly kept track of shipping up and down the Scheldt.

Now that she knew about this, what should she do? Confront him about it? Or simply wait, hoping he would tell her someday? Never before had her trust in Gerrit been so badly shaken.

By evening she still had not decided whether she would confront him. And then he came home with a story so extraordinary that she completely forgot about those four guilders.

"What a day!" he exclaimed, slumping onto the bench. "It seems we're into harboring fugitives now."

"Fugitives?" She came and sat nearby.

"Remember that ship I told you about last night? The one bringing the iron parts we ordered, and the wool we planned to unload as well, even though the ship's master had thought to take it to England?"

"Yes, I remember."

"Both Jorg and I were down on the dock, supervising the unloading. Our stevedores were bringing bale after bale from the hold. Suddenly one of them scrambled up empty-handed. He looked kind of pale and shaken. 'There are people down there,' he said. 'They were hidden among the bales. A whole family—father, mother, and five children. The man told me they were fleeing to England. He seemed a bit disconcerted that the ship was being unloaded at Antwerp.'"

"Were they Mennonites?" Bettgen asked.

Gerrit nodded. "They admitted it right away when Jorg started questioning them. Well, they'd fallen into good hands. You know Jorg. Soft-hearted as a—as a ripe watermelon."

Bettgen couldn't help smiling. "Very poetic, Gerrit!"

He grinned sarcastically. "Not sure why I said that. Anyway, Jorg is putting himself into great danger and taking these people into his home."

"I wish I'd been at the window. I might have seen them arrive."

"Jorg brought them by a back way. He's clever. And he seems to know quite a bit about persecution in the different countries of Europe. He asked this Govert Pruys—that's the Mennonite's name—whether he knew that Queen Elizabeth of England had issued an edict against Anabaptists. He wasn't aware of that. Then he said an astounding thing: 'Maybe it is by God's providence that we have arrived at Antwerp.'"

Bettgen shook her head slowly. "How could he call it God's providence, to be brought into the midst of Alba's persecution?"

"I have no idea. That's why I called his statement astounding. But do you know what? Jorg is making all kinds of plans to give this family a safe home."

"Supposing this Govert agrees to stay away from Mennonite meetings, he could be relatively safe in Antwerp," Bettgen mused. "It's usually at those illegal meetings where the authorities capture the Mennonites."

Gerrit shrugged. "I didn't hear Jorg asking Govert to stop being a Mennonite. But he was offering him work, and a place to stay. And that last bit actually involves you and me."

"Would they move in with us here in the carriage house?"

Bettgen asked with raised eyebrows.

"Where would we put them?" His eyes swept their small quarters. "No, Jorg is urging us to buy that house we've been contemplating. Then the Pruys family could move in here. Jorg seems to think they'd be safer here than if they had a house in town."

"He may be right." Excitement tingled inside her. A real house of their own! So far it had been nothing but a dream—though a dream so real that they had actually gone to view a house for sale, just a short way down the street.

Gerrit put both hands palms down on the table. He seemed to be grappling with a decision. "Jorg says I'm due for a raise. I'm afraid he's being too generous. But a raise would certainly help with paying down a house."

"Why not do it?" she urged. "That house is nice."

He glanced at her. "You like it, don't you?"

Touched by the care in his voice, she nodded. Perhaps he did, after all, occasionally consider her feelings.

"We'll think about it overnight," he decided.

She nodded. "It would be nice if we could help that family. Did you say there are five children?"

"Yes. Two boys and three girls, I think. Two of them were quite small. The oldest couldn't have been more than eleven."

Her heart went out to these hapless children. "Maybe I can meet them tomorrow. Will some of them sleep in the room that had been yours?"

"Could be." He smiled. "Seems Elsa is happiest if she is harboring a vagabond or two."

"Or seven," Bettgen corrected him.

By morning they had decided to accept Jorg's offer for a raise.

Gerrit planned to check in at the house for sale after work.

The minute he had gone, Bettgen crossed the lawn toward the big house. Tryntgen raced to meet her. "You won't believe what has happened!"

"I have some idea, my little niece," Bettgen told her. She still marveled that Elsa's two were now her niece and nephew.

"A whole family came to stay! Father found them on a ship, and they were running away because someone was after them, and we're going to keep them safe." Tryntgen tucked her hand into Bettgen's and walked with her to the door.

"Did you see the baby?" her aunt asked.

"Yes, and she's so cute. Then there's a very little girl, just two years old. And a girl my age, and a boy Ghysbrecht's age, and a bigger girl. But you won't be able to see them. They're all asleep. They haven't even had breakfast yet. Ghysbrecht is hoping the boy will be awake by the time he has done his lessons, so they can play together."

"They'll wake up sometime," Bettgen assured her.

When they entered, the house lay silent. They tiptoed past the spare bedrooms and found Elsa in the drawing room. She had a big bundle of fabric and was studying patterns. Looking up, her first words were, "Bettgen, these people are destitute. They need clothes."

"Show me what to do." Bettgen reached for a pair of scissors.

Soon they heard sounds in the hall. One by one the strangers appeared, the wide-eyed children looking bewildered, scared, and curious all at the same time. Something about the parents—Govert and Lysbet—sent a pang through Bettgen's heart. Was it because they reminded her of the parents she had lost fifteen years ago? No one had given her parents shelter or kept them safe. They had died in prison.

"This is my sister-in-law, Bettgen," Elsa said as Lysbet's eyes landed questioningly on her. "She and my brother live in that carriage house we mentioned, but they're going to buy a house. Isn't that right, Bettgen?"

"Yes." Bettgen glanced again at the children's clothes, which hung in tatters upon them. "I'd be happy to help with sewing."

"You are too kind," Lysbet said, echoing words Bettgen herself had used not long ago.

"Breakfast is ready!" came Elsa's brisk decree. "I heard Pavel's trolley. Let me show you to the dining room."

Bettgen followed the baby's large round eyes as her father carried her away. She longed to cuddle the wee morsel.

She had a feeling her life from now on would be filled to the brim.

chapter twelve

No Compromise

Up and down, up and down went three industrious needles, while three women's heads bent over three projects. Lysbet was already arrayed in a new dress of gray wool; she wore it with the air of one who could not believe it was hers. She was sewing a dress for Leentgen, her oldest daughter. Having done much sewing for Jorg's children, Bettgen was in her element as she stitched new trousers for the Pruys boys. Elsa, on the other hand, seemed almost out of place in the old carriage house with her fine dress and sparkling jewels. Though a needle did not fit so well in her unpracticed fingers, she was determined to help make clothes for the destitute family.

Rubbing the back of her neck, Elsa paused and ran her eyes around the room. "It's surprising what can be crammed into this space. I see you've curtained off several corners for the children's bedrooms."

"Yes. They like it, and so do we. Rest assured, we are not calling this place cramped. It's a mansion compared to anything we've had during the last few years." Lysbet peered at the eye of her needle, threading it with spun wool.

"You lived in Amsterdam the last while?" questioned Elsa.

Another nod from Lysbet. "Originally we lived in Leiden, though. We had a weaver's cottage there."

"I grew up in a weaver's cottage too," Elsa informed her.

Lysbet blinked in disbelief. "You did?"

"Yes. My parents were Mennonite. I thought it's about time I tell you."

"My parents were also Mennonite," Bettgen chimed in.

Bewildered, Lysbet looked from one to the other. Then understanding dawned in her eyes. "Your parents were—taken?"

Both Bettgen and Elsa nodded. Bettgen wondered how this news would affect Lysbet.

Not surprisingly, a tear rolled down her cheek. "That is one of our greatest sorrows, to think that our children may become orphans because of—because of our faith." Quickly composing herself, she added, "Though you two look all right now."

"But we didn't stay Mennonite," Bettgen pointed out gently.

Lysbet bowed her head over her sewing. "Oh, it would be our desire that the children come to the true faith and serve the Lord. If only we may stay with them long enough to lead them in the right."

Awkwardness kept Bettgen and Elsa silent. Bettgen wondered inwardly, *What does she mean by the "true faith"? Would Lysbet class my faith as true?* She thought of the restlessness and turmoil that often plagued her heart. Would becoming a Mennonite change all that? Was Lysbet constantly at peace? Hardly, for she had confessed her worries about the children's future.

In her practical way, Elsa began talking about Leiden. "It's not a big city, is it?"

"No. Just a town. There is no harbor; it's miles from the coast, and miles south and west from the great harbor at Amsterdam. It's in the province of Holland, you know; like most of Holland's towns, Leiden has many canals and streams in and around it. A network of dikes keeps the rivers and canals from overflowing their banks."

Bettgen listened in fascination to Lysbet's description of her home town. How would it be to live at a spot where you'd be inundated if the dikes were breached?

Lysbet got up and went to the window. "Oh, I see the children have strayed into the front yard!" Whisking out the door, she quickly herded them to the back yard again. The adults had decided that the children should not play in areas fronting on the street. They knew they could not keep the Pruys family's presence a complete secret, but a few precautions wouldn't hurt.

Picking up her needle, Lysbet resumed the sewing. "We were wondering—had you hoped we would not pursue any fellowship with the Mennonites here in Antwerp?"

Elsa's sewing dropped into her lap. "We—we don't feel we can dictate to you. Of course, everybody knows the danger increases quite a bit if you attend meetings."

"I know. And it puts you and your family in danger too." Distress clouded Lysbet's face. "But I must confess that Govert has gone several times now. The children and I would like to go too, even though we realize that a whole family on the streets at night is more conspicuous than just one man."

The needle in Bettgen's hand trembled. So these people were persisting in their—their heretical practices! She had hoped they wouldn't. Couldn't they value their lives enough to keep safe? What made them do such dangerous things, when their benefactors were also endangered thereby?

Lysbet was saying, "Followers of Jesus need to meet. Christ is the Head of the body; we are members of His body. Fellowship is so important."

Bettgen faintly remembered her own parents speaking this way. But the intervening years had wiped out any true understanding of what it meant. "We're glad if you can be discreet," she said pointedly.

"If our actions are an offense to you, then we must stop taking advantage of your hospitality and move elsewhere," Lysbet said firmly.

That brought a quick exclamation from Elsa. "We want you to stay! Hopefully we can come to a compromise, where you do all you can to stay hidden, and we do all we can to shelter you."

"Compromise," Lysbet repeated softly. "That word isn't found in Christ's teachings. Either your life is wholeheartedly surrendered to His cross, or..." Her voice trailed off. Obviously she did not want to offend these ladies who were doing so much for her.

Bettgen admitted, "I find it hard to understand how you can surrender yourselves so completely. As though death holds no terror for you."

"It doesn't," came Lysbet's swift reply. "Because of what Jesus did for us on the cross, we can face death with a glad heart, trusting in our Saviour's forgiving love. But we must allow the cross to pierce our hearts and crucify the flesh. That's what makes it possible to follow Christ in truth. In baptism we become one with the death of Christ, meaning the cross frees us from our troublesome flesh."

"So you never have fears or doubts or worries anymore?" Bettgen asked impulsively.

A sad smile crossed Lysbet's face. "As long as we live, we must deal with our flesh daily. But we truly believe Jesus died to free us from the flesh."

"I guess you're not that much different from the rest of us," Bettgen muttered.

"No, we are all alike in our struggles," Lysbet agreed. "Yet when Jesus draws us to Himself, we cannot turn back."

Elsa said thoughtfully, "You have given us some insight into why you live as you do. I believe my parents would have agreed with everything you said."

"We appreciate that you try to understand," Lysbet responded.

Bettgen's mind was still full of questions. *Perhaps*, she thought, *I can ask Leentgen a few questions this afternoon.* The soil was finally dry. Right after dinner, Bettgen wanted to start planting Elsa's garden with the help of the oldest Pruys girl.

Carefully dropping seeds, Leentgen admitted, "I haven't helped with planting since I was a very little girl. In Leiden we used to have a garden, but not in Amsterdam."

"Had you moved to Amsterdam because it was safer there?" Bettgen questioned.

Leentgen's blue eyes clouded. "I think that was the reason. A lot of Mennonites live in Amsterdam. But one day Father found out the authorities want to capture him. So a kind captain allowed us to hide among the bales of wool on his ship—and here we are in Antwerp."

Bettgen dropped some wrinkled pea seeds into her row. "Your mother says you would like to attend a Mennonite meeting here."

"Oh, yes! We miss the meetings," she responded eagerly.

"But aren't you afraid you'll get caught?" That was Bettgen's biggest question: How did the children feel about this fugitive life?

"That's why we moved," Leentgen reminded her. "Here we are strangers, so we hope no one will suspect us. That makes it safer, doesn't it?"

Astonished by the girl's naive words, Bettgen hardly knew what to say. "I—I hope so." Not wanting to strike fear into the child's heart, she changed the subject and began asking questions about their life in Leiden.

A few days later as the two of them again worked in Elsa's garden, Leentgen reported happily, "We went to a meeting last night. It was in the old stables at the Steen castle." Almost before the words were out, she clapped a hand over her mouth. "I shouldn't have said that!"

Bettgen suppressed a smile. "Why not?"

"Because the meeting locations are supposed to stay secret."

"You can trust me," Bettgen assured her. "The last thing I'd want to do is betray you in any way. I don't know if your mother told you, but when I was your age my parents were Mennonites too."

"Oh! Then you know how it is. Where are your parents now?"

Instantly Bettgen wished she had not said that. But there was no denying the truth. "They were captured," she replied, as gently as she could.

"Oh." This time, Leentgen's voice sounded strangled. In silence she went on planting. Then, looking up, she exclaimed, "Here comes Tryntgen. Maybe I shouldn't tell her about the meeting."

"Maybe not. I'm sure she wouldn't do anything to hurt you either—but if ever someone were to question her, it would be easier if she knew nothing about it." Bettgen's heart went out to Leentgen. Poor child! Not yet twelve years old, yet burdened with such heavy secrets.

chapter thirteen

Don't Pressure Me

"Bettgen! A wonderful thing has happened!" Gerrit's face was aglow when he arrived home from work that evening in April.

Relishing his childlike excitement, she asked, "Can I guess?"

"I doubt it. The Sea Beggars have taken a town in South Holland! Prince William's flag is flying over the port of Briel!"

"Oh," she said. "I'd almost forgotten about the Sea Beggars. So they're still around."

"Still around?" Reproach flashed from his eyes. "Did you think they'd all give up the cause for Dutch freedom, just because I've deserted them?"

Unsure how to respond, Bettgen carefully set bowls on the table. "All I meant was that I hadn't been thinking about them." Inwardly she added, "But you obviously have."

"Prince William is planning to attack the Spanish again this summer. It will give him a big boost to hear that the Sea Beggars have started the campaign. Knowing them, I don't think they'll stop with one town. They'll move on to other ports, driving out the Spanish as they go. Mark my words, Bettgen. The year of 1572 is going to be a good year for Prince William!" Gerrit could barely settle down to supper because of his excitement. "Aren't you glad to hear this, Bettgen?"

"I—I guess. Especially if it will mean the end of this terrible persecution," she faltered.

"Definitely. Prince William wants religious freedom. He wants Calvinists and Catholics to exist in peace."

Methodically she spread butter on her slice of bread. "But what about the Mennonites? Can William bring peace to them as well?"

"I would hope so." Gerrit, too, reached for a piece of bread and began to butter it. "Bettgen, I've been doing something behind your back. I feel it's time to tell you about it. Ever since we married, I've been sending money to the Sea Beggars. Four guilders a month. They need money if they're ever going to win a victory over the Spanish."

Bettgen gulped. She had forgotten about those four guilders. So Gerrit was supporting the Sea Beggars. And she had thought he'd made a clean break with his past. The realization was unsettling, to say the least.

"France has pledged to help William," Gerrit rambled on. "You've heard of the Huguenots? That's the French name for Calvinism. The Huguenots want to help the cause of Calvinism in the Netherlands. Right now the Huguenot leader is on good terms with King Charles of France, and has persuaded him to help William. He is gathering an army in France. William will march into Brabant. His brother Lodewyk will come in farther to the north with another army. The Spanish will be caught in the middle—armies on the east, Sea Beggars on the west. We will send the Duke of Alba packing and install William of Orange as our governor instead!"

"He'd merely be governor? We'd still be under King Philip of Spain?" Bettgen queried.

"That's William's plan. I don't understand why. All along, he has insisted that he does not want to wrest the Netherlands away from King Philip. But he also insists we want to be a free, self-governing country. I'm not sure how he'll manage such a contradiction. Still, I trust William."

"Sounds like people expect William to be the savior of the Netherlands," Bettgen said dryly.

"That's it. We do. No one else can do it. The Calvinists believe William is called of God to be their leader."

"And the Catholics—?" she probed.

He shrugged. "I don't know how they feel, and I don't much care either."

"Nobody would guess that you are a Catholic," she told him with a smile.

"I don't care about that either." His voice was rough. "All I want is for our country to be governed in a fair, decent way. Can't you see that, Bettgen?"

"Yes, I can," she said soothingly. "You know, I wonder how the Mennonites feel about William of Orange."

"You could probably find out. You're forever chatting with that—what's her name?—Lysbet. But don't you go around blabbing about the Prince's battle plans. Maybe I shouldn't have spilled all that out to you."

Defensively she told him, "If I know I'm not supposed to repeat something, I won't."

"I'll take your word for it," he said, and his tone was more of a challenge than an affirmation.

Since the following day was too rainy for gardening, Bettgen sought out Lysbet in the carriage house. "I guess there's still some sewing to be done?" she offered.

"Yes, but I feel so unworthy of your help," came the humble reply.

"I am just so glad I have something to do. Over at our house, life gets lonely," Bettgen admitted.

Lysbet gave her an inquiring glance, but said nothing.

"Gerrit is away at work every day," explained Bettgen. "Last night he came home all excited because the Sea Beggars have taken control of a port town. Did you hear about that?"

"No, we didn't." Lysbet did not sound excited.

"Gerrit says the orange, white, and blue flag of William now flies over the town of Briel."

"I see."

"Don't you think it would be easier for the Mennonites if William were to rule the Netherlands?" Bettgen persisted.

Lysbet raised her eyes from her work. "I don't know. We don't pay much attention to politics. We believe God is sovereign."

"I guess you people don't take part in war."

Lysbet shook her head. "How could we take sides in such earthly affairs? Jesus said His followers are not of the earth. The kingdom of heaven ·reigns in our hearts. We leave earthly kingdoms and their struggles in God's hands."

Silently, Bettgen pondered those words. The kingdom of heaven reigned in their hearts. No doubt that was a key to the peace these people knew. Would she ever know a peace like theirs?

Throughout that spring, more news came from the provinces

of Zealand and Holland. Gerrit exulted one evening, "We're finally getting the uprising William needs! Quite a number of towns have declared loyalty to the prince. Haarlem—Alkmaar—Enkhuizen—it's just one after the other. Oh, I like to picture that orange, white, and blue flag fluttering above so many Dutch town halls!"

On impulse Bettgen asked, "Do you know how Govert feels about all this?"

"He's the strangest character," Gerrit said with a shake of his head. "You'd think he'd be elated at the thought of persecution ending. But when I spoke with him alone the other day, he kept saying that Christ's kingdom is not of this earth."

"That's how Lysbet talks too." Bettgen was silent, thinking it over. "Really, though, is their way so strange to us? Wouldn't our parents have said the same?"

"Maybe," he answered shortly.

Even though she sensed he was not in the mood to discuss these things, Bettgen plunged on. "I remember one time when you sounded sort of wistful about our Mennonite heritage, and I suggested maybe we could pursue it. That time, you flatly said we can't, because there's no future for the Mennonites. But if William is made governor of the Netherlands, that could change—right?"

"It could."

His entire body language showed that he was not interested in this subject. Still Bettgen persisted. She had such a longing to share—truly share—with her husband. Lately she had been thinking that if she would bare her heart to him more often, he would open up in return. "Gerrit, sometimes when I'm talking with Lysbet I get this feeling that I'm—that I'm lost. Sinful. Not right with God. Do you—do you ever get such feelings?"

"Bettgen." His voice was ominous. "I know what you're trying to do. You're pressuring me to consider becoming a Mennonite. Get this straight, Bettgen. It will never happen, and I don't want to hear another word about it from you."

"I didn't know I was pressuring you," she whimpered.

"Sorry. I guess it's a sore spot with me, and I get worked up." His apology sounded sincere. "Look, Bettgen. If we were too cowardly to join them while they were a persecuted people, we aren't worthy to join them once persecution eases up. We haven't got what it takes."

"I see what you mean," she said sadly. "Complete surrender is not something we want to do."

"You're pressuring me again," he snarled.

She lifted a hand, almost as though warding off a blow. "Gerrit, please. I only want what's best for us."

"And I ask you to leave it to me to decide what that 'best' is." The way he bit off each word left no question whether he meant what he said.

chapter fourteen

A Home for the Children

Bettgen's heart ached. Something was wrong between Gerrit and her. Of that she felt sure. But what was wrong? Gerrit acted so withdrawn. Was something bothering him? What did he have on his mind? What should she be doing differently?

It was very early in the morning, before dawn, and Bettgen lay awake agonizing over these questions. Surely there was something she could do.

Sometimes the smallest things could make a difference. Later as she cooked porridge, Bettgen hatched a plan. After breakfast she proposed cheerfully, "Do you know what, Gerrit? I'm all ready to go to Elsa's. Why don't I walk with you when you head for the Company?" (The "Company" was what they called Jorg's business.)

Gerrit shrugged. "As you like." After a moment he added, "You spend more time at Elsa's and Lysbet's than you do here at home."

That stung. But she kept her voice cheerful. "Seems there's so

· A Home for the Children ·   93

much more work over there, now that the garden has started. Always hoeing and weeding and planting to be done."

His only reply was a grunt as he reached down to tie his shoes. Quickly she got her hat and shawl. She had to stretch her legs to keep up with his long strides. It took only a few minutes to arrive at Elsa's house, but all the way there Bettgen chattered about the Pruys children. "The baby has grown a lot chubbier. And the two-year-old has lost that scared look in her eyes. She trusts me now." She tried not to mind when Gerrit barely responded. At least she was trying to relate to him. She had to keep trying. Hopefully Gerrit would snap out of the gloom that constantly enveloped him these days.

Bettgen peeked first into the carriage house. It was empty. Her heart raced. What if—? But no, the place was all tidy and clear. If—if bailiffs had burst in, there would be disorder.

Maybe all of them are over at the big house, Bettgen thought as she exited the back door. No children were in sight anywhere. Often at this time of day the babies would still have been at breakfast. Bettgen's sense of foreboding heightened.

No, she would not use the kitchen door at the big house. She had no desire to meet Irema. Going around to the side door—which she knew opened into the drawing room—Bettgen knocked hesitantly.

Elsa was soon there, smilingly commenting on her earliness. "I walked with Gerrit," Bettgen explained. "Would you know, have the Pruys gone to a meeting?"

A frown creased Elsa's forehead. "They do sometimes leave very early—like four o'clock—and stay away all day, not returning till after dark. Usually, though, Lysbet tells me if that's the plan. So you checked there, and they're gone?"

"Every one of them."

"Come on inside," Elsa invited. "Let's not get alarmed. Because of their need to stay hidden, it's no wonder we can't keep track of their doings."

Instead of stepping inside, however, Bettgen said, "I have work in the garden. I just thought I'd see if you know their whereabouts." Picking up her hoe, she began weeding a row of onions. Every minute or so she glanced expectantly toward the Pruys's house.

By dinner she felt she had to do something. Knocking again at Elsa's door, she asked, "Does Govert usually tell Jorg if he's going to be away from work all day?"

"Yes, he does—though that rarely happens on a weekday. The all-day meetings are usually on Sundays," came Elsa's worried reply. "Maybe I should go over to the Company and ask Jorg what he knows about Govert's plans."

"Let me go. I'd talk with Gerrit," Bettgen offered. "Tryntgen and Ghysbrecht would worry needlessly if you suddenly went off to the Company."

"All right. Good idea. But take care, Bettgen. The bailiffs are so suspicious these days," Elsa cautioned.

Bettgen promised, "I'll try not to look suspicious."

Head held high, she walked down toward the river. Once before she had visited the Company. Would she remember where to find Gerrit? He was somewhere on the third floor, that she knew. A young worker gave her directions, and before long she tapped lightly on the door of Gerrit's office.

"Bettgen!" he exclaimed in astonishment. "What brings you here?"

"I'm worried about the Pruys family. They're not at home. Do you have track of Govert? Does he tell you when they're having all-day meetings?" Her words came out in a rush.

"Yes, he and I work together a lot. I'd be surprised if he wouldn't let me know when he plans to be absent for a day." Gerrit frowned. "He definitely isn't here today."

Bettgen's hand went unbidden to her throat. "Oh, I'm afraid they've been to a meeting and were captured."

Gerrit's fingers drummed on his writing table. "Should we be surprised if it has happened? Not that I'd wish it on them. But the choice is theirs. They were fully aware of the Duke's activities, yet they chose to attend meetings—"

"I know, Gerrit. There's not much we can do about Govert and Lysbet, except hope they recant. It's the children that are on my mind. I remember so well how it was—Father and Mother in prison, and we children taken to a convent for questioning. And baptism. They baptized my younger siblings on the very day my parents were taken."

Gerrit's face softened. No doubt the memories were coming back for him as well. "But still, what could we do for the Pruys children?"

"I thought—I thought if someone were to claim them right away, well, maybe it would be a little easier. The children know me. Those babies—they are so afraid of strangers!"

He blinked twice. "You are suggesting we take that whole tribe into our little house?"

"Well, I..." Her heart sank. She had hoped he would agree. "Please, Gerrit. I just feel I must. It's like God is telling me to go find those children."

Picking up a quill, he began writing. After a while he looked up. "I feel we should keep our noses out of this mess. But it seems I can't tell you what to do."

"May I at least go to Father Hoogeveen and see if he knows anything about the children?" She wrung her hands pleadingly.

His eyes were cold. So was his voice. "If you must, then go and do it. Don't forget, though—I'm not recommending it."

"Oh, thank you, Gerrit," she gushed, even while realizing how grudging his permission was. "I'll go and see the priest right away."

"Do be careful," he called after her.

That made her feel a little better. He did care. He just didn't want to make a fuss.

Deep down, she had hoped he would offer to go with her. The fact that he didn't showed how opposed he was to her plan. Was she wrong to go ahead without his whole-hearted approval? But oh—those children!

By the time she reached Father Hoogeveen's residence near the cathedral, her breath came in gasps. She paused at the gate to compose herself, then bravely rang a bell to summon the doorkeeper.

Father Hoogeveen was not as surprised to see her as Gerrit had been. He was a gentle soul who liked to help his parishioners in any way he could. Giving her a chair, he asked what he could do for her.

"I came to see if you know anything about Govert and Lysbet Pruys. Especially about their children." Bettgen had decided to use a very forthright manner in confronting him. If he actually knew something about them, he would hardly be able to hide that fact from her.

Sure enough, there it was—a flicker across his eyes, as though startled at this inquiry about people he had recently seen. But his response was extremely guarded. "Bettgen, I do wonder why you ask me such a thing."

"Because I know those children well! I've been with them every day for weeks. And also because I know exactly what they must be going through—if what I fear is true. Have the parents been imprisoned by the inquisitors? Where are the children? Fifteen years ago, I was the girl whose parents were taken. I know what it's like. I just want to help the Pruys children. Please, Father Hoogeveen, be honest with me."

The guarded look melted from his eyes. "I believe all you're saying, Bettgen. I'm not supposed to be giving such information to anyone, but you have put me on a spot. How could I refuse you?"

"Where are they?" she asked breathlessly when he paused.

"I just got done baptizing those children an hour ago."

"Oh!" A stab of disappointment went through her. And then she wondered why. What was wrong about receiving a Catholic baptism? Now the children were safe; saved by the sacrament of baptism.

But still…an ache remained in her heart. It was not what Govert and Lysbet had wanted for their children. They had wanted their children to reach accountability, then individually choose to follow Jesus.

"Who is with them?" she persisted. "The two babies must be so scared. Please…they would know me…"

"What are you proposing to do, Bettgen?" came his practical question.

Without hesitation she answered, "I would take them home and care for them as if they were our own children."

"And Gerrit knows about this?"

"I went to see him before I came here."

"He gave you permission to come?"

"He didn't say I may not."

Father Hoogeveen sighed. "But it is as I feared—Gerrit has some reservations about this generous plan of yours?"

"Well, some, I guess. But he'll see it differently once we have the children." She spoke with more confidence than she felt. "Father Hoogeveen, you know that Gerrit had a similar experience, only he wasn't baptized until years later."

Father Hoogeveen nodded thoughtfully. "Let me go and talk with a few people. Will you be all right here? It may take some time. I'll ask the housekeeper to bring you some tea."

"Thanks." Bettgen watched the priest leave. Minutes later a woman glided in with a teapot and wordlessly poured some tea into a cup. Again Bettgen said thank you as she accepted it.

Time crawled by. At last she heard footsteps in the hall. More than one set of footsteps. And a baby's cry! She recognized little Emily's voice immediately. And even before the door opened, she thought she heard a sob from two-year-old Janneken.

Trembling, she rose to her feet. Father Hoogeveen was leading Janneken by the hand. On his left arm he carried the unhappy baby. Upon spying Bettgen, the two boys let out squeals of delight. A beautiful smile suffused Leentgen's tear-stained face.

Bettgen reached up. The baby fairly leaped from the priest's arms into hers. Soon both babies were pressed to Bettgen's heart, while the other three stood close.

Father Hoogeveen turned and spoke to the man who had followed him into the room. "It seems we have our answer."

· Open the Dikes ·

chapter fifteen

Tinderbox

"Aunt Bettgen—?"

"Yes, Leentgen."

The twelve-year-old was on her knees picking berries. For a long moment she stared down into her half-filled pail. Then she raised troubled eyes to meet Bettgen's. "Does Uncle Gerrit not like us?"

Pain sliced through Bettgen's middle. Pain for this perceptive girl, who had known far too much pain already; and also pain for the awkward situation that forced her to ask such a question.

When the Pruys children first came into their home, Bettgen had instructed them to call Gerrit and herself Aunt and Uncle. Now she sometimes wondered whether that had been a good idea. Yet she hated to make them change. Their life held enough instability.

How should she respond to Leentgen's question? Gently she asked, "Do you feel Uncle Gerrit is not nice to you?"

Leentgen shook her head. "It's not that, exactly. We just—well, it's like we are in his way. Once he nearly fell over Emily when she was crawling on the floor. He grumbled about that. And I guess maybe Emily disturbs his sleep at night."

Bettgen found herself wanting to squirm. Leentgen was right. Gerrit resented the children's presence. He had not really been in it to take them, and he was not ashamed to let that show. Bettgen had hoped his attitude would change in time, but so far nothing much had changed.

She could still hope, though. To Leentgen she said, "Uncle Gerrit is still getting used to having children around. He has never before known what it's like. Growing up, it was just him and Elsa. No babies. No toddlers."

"You're saying he will get used to it then?" Leentgen persisted anxiously.

"I hope and pray he will. He does like you, in his own way. You've seen him hold the baby, " Bettgen reminded her.

"Y-yes ..." Leentgen's voice trailed off on a doubtful note.

"Also," Bettgen rushed on, "Uncle Gerrit notices what a good help you are with the younger ones. He appreciates that." In her heart, though, Bettgen realized that Gerrit's appreciation for Leentgen's help was mainly because he did not want to help.

Memories crowded Bettgen's thoughts. Mostly she preferred not to relive those first hectic days after the children's arrival. There had been a lot of crying. All the children missed their parents so intensely, and asked many anguished questions. The baby, of course, had cried the most. But that was better now. Emily was after all a year old and could do quite well without her mother.

"Leentgen, even if Uncle Gerrit seems to have a hard time adjusting, never forget how much I love you all, how much I'm enjoying to have you. I'll be sorry when your parents claim you again." Bettgen moved forward along the berry row, struggling to keep pace with Leentgen's nimble fingers.

The girl's picking halted abruptly. "You really think they will be let out of prison?" Her voice was a mixture of disbelief and longing.

"Why not?" Bettgen asked. "All they'd have to do is recant."

"Oh, surely they will not do that!" Leentgen exclaimed in horror.

Bettgen stared in amazement. "You don't want your parents to go free?"

"Well, yes—but not because of recanting. That would mean they denied Christ."

It was almost more than Bettgen could absorb. This slip of a girl already had so much depth that she didn't want her parents to lose faith!

And yet, if Bettgen thought back to her own young days, she could understand why this was so. She too remembered the tears her parents had shed whenever a church brother or sister became weak enough to renounce the faith. Deeply ingrained into the children of Mennonites was the importance of remaining steadfast—at any cost. Yes, even if the price was helpless, orphaned children.

"I'm sorry, Leentgen, I shouldn't have said that," Bettgen apologized.

Leentgen did not reply. Bettgen could only guess at the huge conflict going on in the child's mind. On the one hand was the painful longing to be with her parents again; on the other hand was a barely comprehended desire that they should remain faithful. What a load for such a young girl to bear. But what could she say to help? Leentgen's faith in God seemed sturdier than her own.

From the lower end of the garden came a faint cry. "Emily's awake!" Bettgen exclaimed, hurrying down between the rows to the baby. Arms flailing, Emily tearfully struggled to climb the sides of the basket in which she had taken her nap. "There, there," soothed Bettgen. Gathering Emily into her arms, she sat down on the grass.

Janneken, too, came toddling across the lawn to Bettgen's side. She had been playing in the back yard with Tryntgen and the boys, but she must have heard the baby's cry. The boys followed, and soon all four of the younger children sat close by. Bettgen's heart swelled with emotion. If Gerrit could only have a fraction of the love she felt for these children!

That evening when Gerrit came home he was his usual preoccupied self—with one difference. He told Bettgen what was on his mind. Seeming quite pleased, he began, "It has happened. The northern provinces have declared in parliament that the Prince of Orange is now their governor."

Bettgen reached across the table to help Janneken scrape up the last of her soup. "So you're saying the northern provinces are standing together against Prince Philip."

Gerrit ladled some more soup into his bowl. "They're standing together, yes, and saying they will govern themselves now. However, they still claim to be under King Philip."

"I can never understand that. They declare freedom from Alba, the Spanish governor, yet they still profess allegiance to the Spanish king." Bettgen chuckled.

"It's what William wants," Gerrit reminded her. "Here, Wouter, grab this plate of bread."

Looking fearful, Wouter jerked out a hand to take it.

"Pass it on to Leentgen," Gerrit told him irritably when the seven-year-old sat there holding the plate as though unsure what to do next. Turning again to his wife, Gerrit went on, "The parliament met from July 17 to July 23 at Dordrecht. A proposal was put forth that Calvinists and Catholics should have equal rights."

"What about Mennonites?" The question popped from Bettgen's mouth before she had time to think.

"There was some discussion on that." Gerrit glanced toward Leentgen, who was listening wide-eyed. "William wants religious freedom. He insists no one should be hindered in preaching the Word of God. But others say the persecution of Mennonites must continue. There are also some who want to recognize only the Calvinists and not the Catholics."

"Then they still have some differences to iron out." Bettgen felt disapointed. Why couldn't everyone just agree to the Prince's magnanimous insights?

"I believe William is a man ahead of his time," Gerrit declared. "In the future I think we will see many different denominations existing peacefully side by side. That is the Prince's vision, but it seems a lot of leaders are still too blinded by the old ways. One government, one church. It's the only way they can picture peace and unity in a land."

"Yet has this policy ever resulted in true peace and unity?" wondered Bettgen.

Gerrit shook his head. "Not really. It only brings intolerance—inquisition—persecution. Take France, for instance. You know the French are having a huge struggle as the Huguenots call for equality with the Catholics. Some think the equality might actually come about; the French King Charles has been quite friendly toward the Huguenots. I think that's why Lodewyk was able to gather a French army and enter the Netherlands' southern provinces in a bid to defeat the Duke of Alba."

"Lodewyk. That's Prince William's brother, right? Is he making progress, then?" Though she did not care a great deal about these political goings-on, Bettgen tried to show an interest. Conversations with her husband were rare enough that she wanted to sustain this one.

"Oh, not the best," Gerrit said in reply to her question about the progress of Lodewyk. "His army is stuck in the town of Mons since May, besieged by the Spanish. But at least this has kept Alba occupied so that he couldn't go north and stop the revolution going on up there. Watch it, Janneken! You're spilling your water!"

Bettgen hurried to wipe up the mess. "If the Huguenots were to gain equal rights in France, that would probably affect the rights of Calvinists here."

"Possibly. But, as I was going to tell you when I started talking about France, I feel that land is a tinderbox about to burst into flame. The Catholics hate the Huguenots so much... Oh, Henry!" Gerrit interrupted himself as the five-year-old tumbled from the bench. "Why must you be so restless, anyway?" Gerrit watched moodily as Bettgen rescued the whimpering lad from the floor.

Later, after the children were all asleep, Gerrit admitted, "Sometimes I feel I should be out there helping with the struggle for freedom".

"Oh, Gerrit! You mean, go out and fight with William's army?" gasped Bettgen.

"Or with the Sea Beggars."

"But you are scarcely recovered from that bad wound," she protested.

His objection came swiftly. "I'm as strong as I ever was."

"Gerrit, the children and I need you here," she pleaded.

"You were the one who brought them here," came his muttered reply.

All Bettgen could think was, *He has no idea how much pain he is causing for me.*

chapter sixteen

Poor Lambs

"Do you think it will really happen, Aunt Bettgen?" questioned Leentgen the next day as they busily picked vegetables in Elsa's garden. "I mean—the Prince's idea of religious freedom. Could it happen in the Netherlands?"

Bettgen glanced at the girl's hopeful face. "That would be wonderful, wouldn't it? But I doubt if it will happen anytime soon. The rulers are not in agreement about these things."

"Then it'll probably be too late. Too late to save Father and Mother," Leentgen said sadly.

The familiar ache was back in Bettgen's heart. Oh, these innocent victims! Did those rulers who fought and argued have any concept of the lives and homes they destroyed with their bickering?

"Aunt Bettgen! Janneken woke up now," called Wouter from the carriage house. The two-year-old had been rather grumpy earlier, so Bettgen had ended up putting her down for a nap in the little bed that had been hers before. Janneken seemed to take comfort in the familiarity of the carriage house, where she had lived with her parents.

"No doubt Emily will wake now too. Let's both go in," Bettgen suggested to Leentgen.

As it turned out then, Bettgen was in the carriage house with all five Pruys children when a knock sounded on the door. She opened—and something smote her heart.

The man who stood there was undoubtedly one of the Mennonites. Gravity covered his face. His eyes went around the room, taking in each of the children.

"I had been given an address down the street," he began. "But nobody was at home there. So I thought I'd try the place where Brother Govert and Sister Lysbet used to live."

"Used to live." Bettgen's heart sank further.

He went on, "You are Bettgen Verwest—er, Lieven, I believe?"

Bettgen nodded. Just the way he said it told her that he knew about her past, knew she could sympathize with these children.

"Brother Govert and Sister Lysbet have given their lives for their faith," he said simply.

For a moment Bettgen stood numb. Then, as she went to comfort the weeping Leentgen, her own tears began. The boys' eyes were wide and solemn. Even Janneken sniffled, sensing the grief. But Emily, secure in Aunt Bettgen's arms, cooed and smiled.

"Here," went on their visitor, drawing a folded paper from his vest. "Children, your parents wrote a letter for you." He handed the paper to Bettgen. "Let us know if there is anything you need." With that, he left.

Like rain clouds whose moisture is spent, the weeping in that carriage house gradually died down. Bettgen stared at the paper in her hand. "I can't read, but Uncle Gerrit will read this to you."

"Not today." Leentgen wiped her eyes. "Maybe sometime, but not yet."

"I understand," Bettgen said gently. "Shall we go home now?"

"The vegetables we picked—they're still sitting in the garden," Leentgen reminded her.

Surprised at this practicality in the midst of grief, Bettgen said, "I guess we should take them in to the kitchen."

And meet the cook? She recoiled from the thought. Actually, she and Irema had met a few times this summer, and it hadn't been too bad. But today of all days, with five grief-stricken children in her care, she did not need any scathing words.

Together the six of them picked up the vegetables and carried them toward the house. Before they reached the kitchen, though, Elsa emerged from the side door.

One searching glance at Bettgen's face was all she needed to grasp the situation. Quite likely she had noticed the stranger visiting the carriage house. "Are you heading for home?" she asked kindly. "I could come with you. Jorg and Gerrit won't be home for another hour or so. You'll need some of these vegetables for supper, won't you?"

Though Elsa said very little, her presence helped. She cuddled Janneken and Emily on her lap while Bettgen got supper. The boys trailed disconsolately after Leentgen as she placed bowls, knives, and spoons on the table. This was quite unlike them—but their life had been forever changed. Nothing would ever be the same again for these orphans.

Watching Elsa, Bettgen wondered, *Is this bringing back her memories too?* For the children's sake, though, she kept her thoughts to herself. Another thing she would have liked to ask Elsa was what to do when Gerrit came home. Should she tell him the news in front of the children? Or let him remain ignorant until later when they were alone?

She chose the latter. Elsa was just leaving when Gerrit appeared at the door. Though he gave her a puzzled glance, he asked no questions.

If only he would look deeply into my eyes, yearned Bettgen, *he might realize that something is wrong.* But she knew only too well that Gerrit tended to avoid her eyes.

They started eating. Did he notice that the children were abnormally subdued? That they picked at their food?

As it turned out, however, he took the silence as an opportunity for him to relate his own news without interruption. "I was right when I predicted that France is like a tinderbox ready to burst into flame," he began.

Bettgen wanted to warn, "Please don't talk about tragedies tonight." But she didn't dare.

"I'd told you that Charles, king of France, was growing quite friendly with Coligny, the Huguenot leader," Gerrit continued. "But Catherine, the king's mother, didn't like that at all. So she agreed to a Catholic plot to kill Coligny. That was on Aug. 22. Things didn't work out, though; Coligny was only wounded. Now Catherine was in a desperate spot. She didn't want her part in the plot to become known. So she had the king order the death of all the other Huguenot leaders. Apparently she persuaded Charles that they'd been plotting against him.

"Quite a lot of Huguenot leaders happened to be in Paris right then for a royal wedding. So on the morning of Aug. 24—which is the feast of Saint Bartholemew, if you know anything about that—the Huguenot leaders were assassinated. That really set off the Catholics everywhere. They began murdering Huguenots by the hundreds. Maybe thousands. That was over a week ago, and they say the killing is still going on."

Bettgen held a hand over her face. "Oh, Gerrit," was all she managed to say. The story was too much for hearts raw with grief.

But Gerrit was still oblivious to their pain. He began speculating what the events in France would do to the war here in the Netherlands. "Lodewyk was depending on more help from France. He isn't going to get it now. If Charles is killing Protestants in his own land, why would he send aid to Protestants in another land? I'm guessing the Duke of Alba can now easily defeat Lodewyk. And I can guess what Alba will do next. He'll storm north with his army and try to take back the provinces that have declared William as their leader."

"So much war," Bettgen said faintly. How could she stop Gerrit from relating any more horrible news?

Whether he had run out of things to tell, or whether he realized that something was wrong, Gerrit did fall silent now.

Once Bettgen had told him the news about Govert and Lysbet in the darkness of their bedroom, he muttered, "I thought the children were pretty quiet at the supper table."

"The poor lambs," Bettgen said. "And it's all so vivid for me too, because of my memories. Yours too, I guess."

There was no reply. After tossing and turning for a while, he burst out, "Are we stuck with these children now?"

"We're all they have," she whispered.

"Some Mennonite family could take them in."

"It wouldn't work. The only reason the authorities let them come here rather than to the convent was because we're Catholic."

"They could go to the convent, then."

"Gerrit…"

"Sounds like you're pretty set on keeping them," he snarled.

"I hate to disrupt their lives even more. They've learned to call us Aunt and Uncle ... this is the only home they know..."

No reply. More tossing and turning. Then he spoke again, this time with a change of subject. "If what I suspect is true—that Alba will now attack the Calvinist cities up north—I feel even more strongly that they need all the help they can get."

Now it was her turn to remain silent. What could she say? Pleading with him to stay home would not help—would, in fact, work the wrong way. But somehow, somehow, she must make him see how much she needed him.

A sound came from the small room next to theirs. "I think I hear Henry crying," she said.

She waited, wishing—hoping—Gerrit would go to comfort the five-year-old. Surely he could not harden his heart against a fatherless little boy.

"Why don't you go and quiet him down?" asked Gerrit in a muffled voice.

She went, and her heart was bleeding—for more reasons than one.

chapter seventeen

Restless

Bettgen opened one eye. The room was gray; that meant dawn had broken. Sunday morning was here, and she still had no answer for her question.

Gerrit was no help. When she asked him, "Don't you think I should take the children to Mass?" he had shrugged and replied, "Whatever you wish." What she really wished was to discuss it with him. Tell him that she felt the Pruys children ought to have a worship experience. At the same time she would have to admit that she wondered whether she'd betray them by taking them to a Catholic service. Their parents would not have approved...

But Bettgen didn't even try to talk it over with Gerrit. Where the children were concerned, he remained so totally uninterested that she felt like crying. The only topic truly interesting to him was the progress of the Dutch revolt. In late October he'd been all excited about the fact that Prince William of Orange had gone to Holland. Not with an army, because he no longer had one. He'd gone simply because the people pleaded with him to come and be with them.

Holland and Zealand were in desperate straits this fall. Just as Gerrit had predicted, the defeat of Lodewyk in the south left the Duke of Alba's armies free to go north. Terrible vengeance was being wreaked upon the cities and towns that had dared to break away from Spanish rule. The Duke's son, Don Frederick of Toledo, was in charge of the army and he had no mercy. With fire and sword, the rebellious towns were cruelly punished. One after the other they surrendered to the bloodthirsty armies of Toledo.

Yet William had agreed to risk his life and enter this bloody turmoil. His care and concern were touching, yes. But still, Bettgen could not become enthused over these goings-on far away to the north. She had too many cares, too many unresolved questions, of her own.

If anything, Gerrit only added to her burdens. She could see that he chafed at the bit, longing to go up there and help the Prince fight Toledo. Bettgen had told him, "It will soon be winter. Surely there won't be much fighting during the cold weather. You would get sick, Gerrit. Imagine sleeping in a tent on the cold ground. If you got sick or—or died, you wouldn't be of any use to the Prince."

Gerrit always had counter-arguments for her pleadings. "The Prince isn't excusing himself. He could get sick too. But he's up there, sleeping in tents like a common soldier. His presence helps to keep the people from discouragement. If they are discouraged, they will surrender. William encourages them to stand fast."

"You are not William," she had reminded him, and he had glowered at her.

Kicking off the blanket, Bettgen leaped out of bed. It was high time she got ready for Mass. As for the children, her mind was made up.

Or so she thought. After breakfast she announced to the five, "You will go to Mass with me."

She was unprepared for the look that came over Leentgen's face. Without hesitation the girl shook her head and said, "We can't."

In a gesture that momentarily reminded her of Irema, Bettgen put her hands on her hips. "Why do you say that?"

"Our parents wouldn't like it." Though soft, Leentgen's voice was laced with steel.

"Your parents are not here." Instantly, Bettgen regretted the cruel words. These children did not need such a reminder.

A tear glistened in Leentgen's eyes. Wouter's head was way down. Henry looked fearfully from one to the other.

"We can't go to Mass," Leentgen repeated, though this time her voice trembled.

"All right," Bettgen relented. "Then I suppose I'll have to stay at home with you. Again. I've missed a lot of Mass the last while." It was horrible, she knew, to take her frustration out on Leentgen. Time and again she had asked Gerrit to stay with the children, for he never went to Mass. But he always refused and went off somewhere else. His attitude was, "You wanted them; you can take care of them." It was true that she wanted them. The only time she felt trapped by their care was when she longed for Mass.

"We can stay by ourselves."

Stunned by the girl's offer, Bettgen realized her mouth hung open. After a moment she shook her head. "I can't leave you alone. I'll stay."

To make up for the turmoil she had caused the children, she tried to make the morning a truly happy one. She played with them and sang to them. The little ones loved it, but Leentgen's response was half-hearted at best. The hurt had gone too deep.

That Monday as Leentgen helped wash clothes in the cellar, she began slowly, "Maybe we could go and live with Jan and Elizabeth."

Bettgen's hands flew out of the suds. "Who's that?"

"We used to see them at meeting. They have no children. I just thought—"

"Leentgen! We—I—want you here," Bettgen interrupted sharply.

A wan smile touched the girl's face. "I'm glad. But it bothers me that you can't go to Mass. And—and Gerrit doesn't want us…"

"He'll learn. He's just getting used to having children around," Bettgen said, more firmly than she felt.

"I really think I could stay with the little ones while you go to Mass on Sunday mornings." Leentgen scrubbed hard at a stain on Emily's dress. "You're only gone for an hour or so."

"We-ell, I'll think about it this week," Bettgen promised.

By the next Sunday she decided to give it a try. The moment Gerrit heard of her plans, he said he was going for a walk along the river. That shattered any hopes she'd entertained of him reconsidering and being the children's guardian while she was gone. Filled with misgivings, she donned her hat and shawl and said good-bye to the children. Emily's whimper at seeing her leave brought a good feeling—which was quickly overwhelmed by worry as she hurried to the cathedral.

All through Mass she fretted. What if Henry or Janneken fell and got hurt? What if Emily cried the whole time she was gone? What if some intruder entered the house? What if—and this was worst of all—someone from the Office of Inquisition came for these children who had been snatched from convent life?

She was panting by the time she reached home. What music for the ears when happy sounds of play floated through the doorway! Everyone was all right. Everyone was happy. But oh, how eagerly Emily came into her arms—as though she'd pined for her "Auntie" the whole time she was gone.

"Next Sunday I'll stay home," Bettgen promised, nuzzling the little one's fine golden hair.

And she did stay home that Sunday. But as the winter wore on, time hung heavily on Bettgen's hands. Day after day she was cooped up with the children. Day after day she listened to their chatter and settled their quarrels. The quarreling was difficult. It left her feeling frayed at the edges. Yet she knew that quarreling was a sign of normalcy. Children who quarreled were children who felt at home.

Elsa did her part to help pass the winter. She frequently invited Bettgen and the children over to the big house. A few times Bettgen returned the invitation, but it seemed their house was too small to hold an extra three people when Elsa brought Tryntgen and Ghysbrecht.

As the year changed to 1573, Bettgen began going to Mass again. For her conscience's sake she did it only every other week. It was surprising how an hour away from the children refreshed her—providing she kept the worry at bay.

Gerrit hated the children's bickering. One morning at breakfast, Wouter began pestering Henry about something. At first Bettgen ignored them, hoping their tiff would blow over. Then Wouter pinched Henry, and he let out a howl.

Bettgen opened her mouth to scold. Suddenly Gerrit lunged to his feet. "Can't a man have any peace in his own home?" Leaving part of his breakfast uneaten, he grabbed his hat and coat. The house shook as he slammed the door behind him.

Needless to say, the quarrel had come to a sudden stop. Which was a good thing, because Bettgen could not have spoken if she'd tried. Sobs were pushing into her throat. As quickly as she dared, she left the table. Mumbling that there was washing to be done, she escaped downstairs. Her tears mingled with the wash water. Would Gerrit never change? Even if it was impossible for him to love the children, couldn't he at least learn to tolerate them?

Amidst the sloshing of her suds, Bettgen heard a voice from above, seeping through cracks in the kitchen floor. Leentgen was talking, her voice so stern and solemn that Bettgen barely recognized it.

"Henry. Wouter. You absolutely must stop making fusses in front of Uncle Gerrit."

The boys' reply was too faint to hear. Leentgen went on, "If you don't stop, we'll get kicked out. All of us. Uncle Gerrit is not going to keep us any longer if you don't quit your quarreling."

"We want to stay!" whimpered Henry.

That made Bettgen smile through her tears. But oh, the poor little boys. Life for them was hard enough without being under a threat. Maybe she should go up and tell Leentgen it wasn't true; that Uncle Gerrit wouldn't kick them out.

But how could she know? Perhaps Leentgen was right.

chapter eighteen

Missing

It was May 10, 1573. When Gerrit came home from work that evening, he seemed unusually burdened. "The city of Haarlem has been under siege by the Spanish for months," he said. "The Spanish pride must be taking a real blow, because when they marched upon Haarlem they boasted of conquering it in seven days or less. Now almost six months have passed and the siege is still on. I certainly admire the brave citizens of Haarlem for holding out!"

Bettgen hardly knew what to say. As usual, news of the war did not really interest her. Yet she so yearned to talk with Gerrit that any conversation seemed worth prolonging. "With all the plundering and murdering done by the Spanish in other cities they conquered, perhaps the Haarlem citizens feel they'd rather die under siege than surrender."

"Maybe so," he agreed. "But there is also hope that the Sea Beggar fleets will come to their aid. In spite of the siege, Haarlem is not completely cut off. Provisions and fresh troops can still be brought in across the Haarlem Lake." As he spoke, Gerrit paced restlessly around the room.

Watching him, Bettgen could all too easily guess what he was thinking. He probably wished he were up there, helping those Sea Beggar ships against the Spanish, and perhaps helping to win a glorious victory at Haarlem. Oh, if only Gerrit would take as much interest in the needs right here at home! Had he no idea how rewarding it would be if he truly acted as a father to these fatherless children?

At noon the next day, Bettgen was astonished to find Jorg standing on her doorstep. Why would the busy owner of a large company come to see her? From his face she knew instantly that something was wrong.

She invited Jorg inside, and he took the chair she offered. Taking out a handkerchief, he wiped his brow. "It's a warm morning out there."

Bettgen could hardly endure the suspense. When was Jorg going to tell her why he'd come?

"About an hour ago," he began carefully, "I went to Gerrit's office because I wished to speak with him. He was not there. I asked a few workers whether they had seen him, but they had not. Finally I noticed a letter lying on his desk. Two letters, actually. One for me and one for you." He handed a paper across to her.

"I can't read," she admitted, her voice trembling as she handed the letter back. "Would you please read it to me?"

He glanced at the children, who stood wide-eyed in a circle. Then, apparently deciding they might as well hear it, he began: "'Bettgen: I have decided to follow my calling. This morning I am taking a boat down the Scheldt which will carry me to a Sea

Beggar ship. I might come back someday. Gerrit.'"

It was like a blow to her face. Bettgen's knees turned weak, and she sat down. Little Janneken and Henry crowded anxiously against her. Even while tears ran down her cheeks, Bettgen put her arms around them. The poor dears had no idea what was wrong.

Jorg cleared his throat. "I'm sorry that I had to bring this news. I would have done anything to keep Gerrit. He is such a good worker. And he was so much needed here too."

"Yes, so needed here," she agreed brokenly. Did Jorg have any idea that this was not altogether a surprise to her? She was not going to tell him. Her pride would not let her.

Awkwardly, Jorg got to his feet. "We hope this war will soon be over, then he can come home. In the meantime..." He paused. "I must talk with Elsa about this, but I'm sure she will agree. You and the children are welcome to return to the carriage house. You would not be so alone there, and we would provide whatever you need."

She wiped her eyes. "Thank you, Jorg. We'll talk about that later."

Taking that as a sign of dismissal, Jorg walked stiffly out the door. For some minutes Bettgen stayed there, hugging Janneken and Henry, while Leentgen held Emily, and Wouter looked on with troubled eyes. Bettgen could have cried on and on. But for the children's sake, she had to compose herself and get dinner.

All day she held back her tears. It was hard—especially when Leentgen asked sadly, "Did he go away because he couldn't stand us children anymore?"

Bettgen groped for words. She did not want to lie; yet neither did she wish Leentgen to feel so burdened. "Oh, Leentgen, I'm sorry you even have to think such a thing. Please stop thinking that way. You heard what the letter said. Gerrit felt he had a calling to go and help the Sea Beggars in the struggle against the Spanish."

"But you are not glad he went," Leentgen persisted.

"How could I be? We wanted him here." Bettgen looked around, wishing she could change the subject and get Leentgen's mind on something else.

"Why did he go away without telling you?"

The unsuspecting girl did not realize that this question was a dagger in Bettgen's heart. "I don't know, Leentgen. Could you please hang these washed clothes on the line?"

Not till that night did Bettgen allow her pent-up tears to flow freely. Even then, she hid under a blanket so no sounds would carry to the next room. "Oh, Gerrit, Gerrit," her heart mourned. "Leentgen fears she is at fault—but really, I'm the one at fault. I pushed you too hard. I wanted my own way, and I got it too. I did not allow you to be the proper head of our household. I thought this idea of taking the Pruys children was so needful, so charitable, that I could push it through even if you did not give your consent. But I should have waited. I should have let you make the decisions. Why can I see that so clearly now? Why couldn't I see it then? I have wrecked our home."

On and on went the tears. For a while it seemed she would cry all night. But at some time she must have fallen asleep, because sunshine surprised her awake some hours later. Dragging herself out of bed, she began another day. The questions nagged her hour by hour. Would Gerrit ever come back? Would she ever get a chance to rectify the mistakes she now could see so clearly?

His letter had been so cold, so very cold. Not "Dear Bettgen," or "To my dear wife." Not even, "From your husband." Just

"Bettgen"—"Gerrit." "I might come back someday," he had written. She wanted to think he only meant he might die before he could return. But something told her that he considered never returning, even if he lived through every battle. "Oh, Gerrit, Gerrit!" her heart mourned.

Elsa did all she could to help. She came over the next morning, and together they made the decision to move back to the carriage house. They even started packing things. The following day, Elsa sent a servant with a wagon. So by afternoon Bettgen and the children were back once more in that familiar cramped space.

Just as Bettgen began cudgeling her weary brain to think about supper for her brood, a knock sounded on the old, cracked door. There stood Irema, one hand on a hip, the other grasping the big iron pot Bettgen remembered well from her kitchen maid days. "Brought you some supper," Irema said, holding the pot forward.

"Thanks," Bettgen said stiffly. Now. Now was the chance Irema had predicted, had possibly been awaiting. "I told you so," she would say. "I warned you not to trust that man."

But Irema said nothing of the sort. Looking deep into Bettgen's eyes, she simply said, "Life goes on. It has to." With that, she turned and stumped back to the kitchen.

Breathing in a lungful of the stew's fragrance, Bettgen carried it to the table. No one could make stews like Irema.

And right now, probably no one knew better than Irema what she was going through. Irema had experience. Her husband had left her too.

Day and night the questions and regrets tormented Bettgen's conscience. Finally she decided to do what any good Catholic would do: she went to confession. Father Hoogeveen was kind, compassionate. He promised her forgiveness of sins and a future home in heaven. With a gently spoken blessing he sent her back to the children, who had stayed with Elsa.

At first Bettgen thought the confession had helped. She felt she could breathe easier. But as time went on she knew the change had not been real—had not penetrated her heart. She still ached with regret. And on some days she still felt angry. Angry at Gerrit for not being the man he should have been. Angry at herself for— oh, so many things.

She lost all desire to attend Mass. One day in July Leentgen offered, "We could stay alone if you want to go to Mass with Jorg and Elsa. Actually, we wouldn't be alone because there are always some servants around."

Bettgen shook her head sadly. "I don't want to go, Leentgen. Thanks for offering. I want to stay with you every minute of every day. You children are all I have."

It was true. Even when nothing else motivated her—not even gardening, which used to be her favorite work—the children's needs kept her going. She cooked for them, sewed for them, cleaned for them. She cheered Wouter on as he learned to read by joining Ghysbrecht's lessons with the tutor. She thrilled to see Wouter coming home and teaching his older sister to read as well. And in the end, Bettgen herself began to learn letters and words. Small bright spots they were, these lessons, in days always overshadowed by the memory of her loss.

chapter nineteen

How Alkmaar Was Saved

"Haarlem has fallen to the Spanish. Had you heard?" Elsa asked one day as she and Bettgen sat sewing in the drawing room of the big house. Through the window they could watch the children at play, carefree in the September sunshine.

"No, I hadn't heard. When did the Spaniards take it?"

"End of June, I think. The siege had lasted seven months."

Bettgen stitched on while questions raced through her mind. Had Gerrit been there at Haarlem? Had he been on the ship that brought provisions to the hard-pressed city? With a hint of sarcasm she said, "So if Gerrit hoped he could help save Haarlem, he must be disappointed."

Elsa chuckled. "I'd say if he thought his presence would make such a difference, it's time his pride received a little prick."

Bettgen sat silent. She was still trying to figure out how Elsa really felt about her brother's defection. Was she angry at him? Even while doing all she could to help her sister-in-law, Elsa had a gift for hiding her true feelings.

"It seems the Spanish became over confident," Elsa continued. "A few days after Haarlem fell to them, a small party of soldiers marched up the coast with intentions of taking Alkmaar. They were in for a surprise. Though Alkmaar is smaller than Haarlem, it was not easily taken. The Beggars helped three times to beat back the Spanish troops. As the weeks went by it looked like there would be another long siege. But Sonoy had a clever plan."

"Who's Sonoy?" wondered Bettgen. Now that her husband was involved, she found herself taking a personal interest in the struggles of Holland.

"He's the governor Prince William chose for North Holland. Anyway, Sonoy's plan was to flood the Spanish army out! Much to the dismay of local farmers, Sonoy cut the dikes and opened sluices until water overran the fields and crept toward the army encampments. That's all it took to send those soldiers packing. Jorg says the Spanish are uneasy at best with all the waterways they must deal with in Holland and Zealand. The sea rolling toward them was more effective than an army of thousands would have been."

A faint memory from her childhood days nudged Bettgen's thoughts. "Isn't there a story in the Bible of a pursuing army that got swallowed by the sea?"

Elsa nodded. "I was thinking the same thing. As a little girl I heard a minister tell the story. But I've mostly forgotten it now."

Bettgen prompted, "So anyway, Alkmaar still belongs to the Prince of Orange?"

"Yes, and more towns are putting up a strong resistance. Even though Haarlem was lost, it seems the Hollanders as a whole are not yet giving up to the Spanish."

Bettgen sighed. "Sometimes I wish they would just give up. This war is dragging on and on."

"I know what you mean." Elsa rose and began cutting fabric for another small garment. "Surely God does not want people to be killing each other like this, all in the name of religion."

Bettgen sent her sister-in-law a startled glance. When had she ever heard Elsa speaking about God in that way?

God. Who really was He? What did He expect from His people? What did He want from her, Bettgen Lieven? Through Catholicism she had been taught that no ordinary person could have a relationship with God. Such things were for the priests, who stood as intermediaries between God and the common man. If an ordinary person prayed, it was usually to the Virgin Mary or some other saint.

Yet because of her childhood, Bettgen knew that was not the Mennonite way. She could remember her father praying to God. Father and Mother had trusted in a loving God who cared about them personally. Their faith had sustained them through capture, interrogation, imprisonment, illness, and death. They had looked forward to glory.

Why could she not have a faith like that? Bettgen wondered. Why was she constantly troubled and oppressed, constantly weighed down by a sense of sin in her life? She had tried the confessional, and it had not really helped. Oh, for freedom! Not the kind of freedom for which Dutchmen were fighting Spaniards, but a freedom of spirit that would deal with sin and lift her above the dreariness and toil of life. Was such a freedom available? Did it lie in those nearly forgotten roots going back to a childhood home where God was worshiped as Father and Savior?

Leentgen, dear girl, was so sensitive to Bettgen's sadness. One day she suggested, "I just thought of something, Aunt Bettgen. We have still not read my parents' letter. Do you think we can read well enough now to do it ourselves? It might cheer us up."

"I'd forgotten about that letter," Bettgen admitted. "But I know exactly where it is." Going to the tiny bedroom, she found the letter in the linen chest that had been Gerrit's gift to her.

All was quiet in the carriage house, for the little ones were at play outside. Together, Bettgen and Leentgen bent their heads over the much-wrinkled paper. Not many minutes passed before Bettgen let out a sigh. "There are so many big words. I guess I can't read very well yet."

"Me neither," Leentgen agreed ruefully. "Still, some parts I can figure out. I can see that Father and Mother were—were looking forward to something beautiful after they leave this earth."

"Yes. But wouldn't you say..." Bettgen pored once more over the handwriting. "Wouldn't you say they also had something beautiful here—even while in the foul dungeon of the Steen castle?"

Leentgen was quick to agree. "Else how could they have borne it all? How could they have remained faithful even when they knew they would be killed?"

Bettgen tapped her fingers on the paper. "I would like to know what that 'something beautiful' was."

After Bettgen went to get dinner, Leentgen kept studying the letter. "It seems to me that Father and Mother wanted to tell me how I can become a child of God," she said some minutes later.

"A child of God?" The thought intrigued Bettgen. Having put the pot on to boil, she came and sat near Leentgen again.

"We have to see how sinful we are, and then..." Leentgen's eyes scanned the paper. "Repent. I'm not sure what that word means.

Father used it many times in this letter. We must repent. And then believe."

"Believe what?" asked Bettgen.

"That—that Jesus forgives. 'Jesus sets us free from sin.' That's what Father wrote. Our ministers say it too." Leentgen looked up. "Aunt Bettgen, if we have so many questions, why don't we go to meeting?"

Bettgen blinked—once, twice, three times. "We'd get caught; that's why. The Duke of Alba's bloodhounds roam the streets. I have no desire to get stuck in the Steen and leave you children alone again."

Leentgen thought for a moment, then said quietly, "Still, I would like to go."

It was unsettling, to say the least. Here was this twelve-year-old, having lost her parents to Alba's Council of Blood—yet she wanted to go to meeting. Bettgen could not shake the thought. It followed her everywhere for over a week. Finally she asked Leentgen, "How would you find out the location of the meeting?"

"I'd go to Jan and Elizabeth and ask them. Jan is a 'wet-doener'—a notifier. He lets people know about the meetings."

"Hmm. Well, I wouldn't let you go see Jan alone. I'd have to go with you," Bettgen decided.

"Would you?" Leentgen's face was radiant.

Bettgen had not the heart to say no. Telling Elsa that she and Leentgen needed to attend the market, they left the children in her care and went. After a quick tour of the market—where they bought only a handful of herbs—they found Jan's home. He and his wife recognized Leentgen right away.

"We've been thinking about you," Elizabeth said warmly. Glancing at Bettgen, she added, "We're so glad you're caring for the children."

"It is my privilege to have them," Bettgen said stiffly. She felt ill at ease and full of misgivings. Why had she agreed to come here?

Once Leentgen realized that "Auntie" wasn't going to make the request, she began, "We thought we'd like to come to meeting, if you would tell us where and when the next one is."

A glad light sprang into Jan's eyes. "There is to be a meeting right here in our house on the next Lord's Day. Starting at 3:30 in the morning."

"So if you're gathering at such an hour, I suppose the police are still bothering you?" Bettgen asked sharply.

Elizabeth leaned forward. "Actually, there have been no incidents recently. It almost seems the Duke is preoccupied with trying to stop the revolt, and isn't so hard on the trail of 'heretics.' But we are still taking precautions."

"I'd suggest that you try not to think about those possibilities." Jan cleared his throat. "Focus instead on seeking the Lord. The Bible promises that God is a rewarder of them that diligently seek Him. When we seek Him, God is right there waiting. Our part is to see our need for Him, and to open our hearts so He can enter. The Bible also speaks of a 'river of water of life, flowing from the throne of God.' A great river of love is waiting to flood the life of one who seeks God."

"Father once helped me memorize those words about 'a rewarder of them that diligently seek Him,'" Leentgen recalled. "But I had forgotten them."

"You will be glad to hear God's Word again," Jan said warmly.

Bettgen, however, was feeling more and more uncomfortable. She rose to her feet. "It's time we went home." Leentgen followed obediently enough, but her reluctance was only too obvious.

Apparently she would have liked to stay for hours.

All the way home, Bettgen walked so fast that Leentgen had a hard time keeping up. Talking was out of the question—which was exactly the way Bettgen wanted it. In her thoughts she berated herself, "Why did you do this? What have you let yourself in for?"

chapter twenty

The Way Forward

Leentgen proved once again how perceptive she was. All evening she said nothing to Bettgen about their afternoon visit at Jan's house. She seemed to know instinctively that Bettgen did not want to discuss it. Not until Friday did she timidly ask, "Will we go to the meeting, Aunt Bettgen?"

Bettgen sighed. Her mind was still in such a turmoil about the matter. Refusing to meet Leentgen's eyes, she replied, "I don't know what to say. I'm worried about what Gerrit would think if he knew I went with you to Jan's place."

Leentgen was silent. Her shoulders drooped as she went outside to check on the children.

Not until Saturday evening did Bettgen make up her mind. "We won't go. Not tomorrow, anyway," she told Leentgen. "I'm just too undecided." She couldn't help feeling sorry for the girl. She looked so disappointed.

Weeks passed—weeks filled with some more indecision and

unhappiness. Bettgen was strongly tempted to ask Elsa for advice. Yet it seemed ridiculous. What advice could she expect from her Catholic sister-in-law other than what her own cautious nature advised her? Attending a Mennonite meeting was just about the foolhardiest thing she could do. Why not forget all about it?

Why not, indeed? Because some things are very hard to forget. When a person opens even a tiny part of her heart to God, He will not easily let go. He will draw and draw with His tender love, which is stronger than human reasoning and human fears.

It was late in November one morning when Elsa related astounding news. "The Duke of Alba has been recalled to Spain!"

"You mean he has actually left the Netherlands?" Bettgen asked in a dazed way.

"Yes. Both he and his son, Don Frederick of Toledo—the one who led the armies up north—have gone home. It seems King Philip was not happy with the way things were going this year. The Sea Beggars have been gaining too many victories. Only a few towns of Holland and Zealand remain in Spanish hands."

"I can hardly believe it. All these years we have lived in the shadow of Alba's Council of Blood. Now, suddenly, he is no longer our governor," Bettgen marveled.

Elsa said, "I surely hope this means the Mennonites can breathe more easily. It's horrible to think how many of them were slain by Alba's Inquisition. I'm amazed that there are any Mennonites left in Antwerp."

Impulsively Bettgen began, "Maybe we could—" Then she stopped. She hadn't really intended to talk about this to Elsa.

Elsa eyed her curiously. "Could what?"

"Oh, I don't know. It's just an idea Leentgen and I were discussing. She and the boys would like very much to attend a meeting." Bettgen watched her sister-in-law's face. When no great astonishment showed, she dared to continue. "I was thinking maybe I should take them sometime."

To her amazement, Elsa agreed. "That might be a good idea. They've lost so much; going to a meeting might be a healing experience."

"I didn't know what you'd think of the idea," Bettgen confessed. "But now that you're encouraging me... Well, Leentgen says Jan and Elizabeth are the folks who know the where and when of meetings."

"I see. So all you'd have to do is contact them. Let me know. I can keep the baby if you like."

"Actually, if we go I'd like to take the little ones," Bettgen decided.

So it came about that one windy night in December, Bettgen attended her first meeting since the one in 1558 when her parents were captured. Even after fourteen years, there was something familiar about it, almost a sense of home-coming. The message was simple and direct, telling of Jesus and His kingdom upon earth, wherein men can live at peace regardless how much the worldly kings raged and fought.

For Bettgen Lieven, however, the battle was not easily won. Agreeing to attend more meetings was easy enough; the children wanted so badly to go. But the battle for her heart was a long, hard tug-of-war. Sin and self encamped like besieging enemies around her, blocking the flow of that great "river of water of life" which brings God's saving love into a heart—providing the door is opened.

There was the matter of the new governor from Spain, for one thing. Don Louis des Requesens seemed a friendlier, less harsh man than the Duke of Alba. Yet he had his orders from King Philip, and they had not changed. Exterminate heresy! Only the Catholic Church was to be allowed in Philip's realm. Would Requesens use the same bloody tactics Alba had? Time would tell.

Bettgen noticed that the Mennonites had few discussions about the new governor. Secure in God's will, they continued to serve and worship in any way they could without needlessly endangering their families. Oh, the women sometimes struggled with worries and concerns. The more Bettgen learned to know the sisters, the more she realized they were not much different from herself.

But they had faith. And where was her faith? Why could she not break free from these shackles and walls that imprisoned her heart?

It happened gradually—so very gradually. Meeting after meeting, Bettgen absorbed the truth of God's Word. Meeting after meeting, her sense of need grew. Meeting after meeting, almost unknown to her, God's love and forgiveness chipped away at the walls. When finally her surrender was complete, and she confessed her willingness to follow Jesus by the way of the cross, Bettgen herself wondered how it had happened. There had been no great earthquake in her soul, no overpowering sensation—but she was ready. Being baptized was the only way forward. The washing of the Word, the "river of water of life," were reality in her heart, and baptism would be the seal of that reality.

How would Elsa react to the news? There was only one way to find out. On a morning in March of 1574 the two of them sat sewing in the drawing room. Through the walls they heard the happy chatter of seven children together at play in the next room. "Elsa, I'm going to start taking instructions for baptism next Sunday," Bettgen told her quietly.

Elsa's sewing dropped into her lap. Bettgen could not quite fathom what she saw in her eyes. It was not surprise, yet neither was it disapproval. Her voice was quiet as she said, "I thought maybe that would happen."

"Are you disappointed in me?" Bettgen wasn't sure why she asked that. No amount of disappointment from Elsa could have changed her mind now.

"No...no. Mostly I admire you."

Bettgen shook her head. "No admiration, please. It's only by the grace of God. On my own it would never have happened. I'm quite the weak person."

"Something tells me, though..." Elsa groped for words. "Something tells me that faith gives strength to a person."

"A strength not one's own," Bettgen agreed. "All praise belongs to God. And sometimes I still wonder... I mean, it seems so foolhardy..."

"We'll do all we can to protect you," came Elsa's swift promise. "And Bettgen, I can't help being wistful. My roots, you know. I can't forget them, just like you couldn't forget yours."

"The roots are not enough, though. Only the love of Jesus can break down the high walls of sin and self. Brother Claes said that not long ago." Bettgen sighed happily. "This is an unexpected blessing, that I can freely talk with you about these things. But Elsa, sometimes I wonder what would happen if—" She could hardly bring herself to say it. "If Gerrit were to come home."

Impulsively, Elsa reached over and touched her hand. "God will still be with you." Then her face reddened. "Who am I to say that?"

"You are my sister-in-law," Bettgen said firmly. "And perhaps God is at work in your heart too." After a pause she added, "Even though I dread what Gerrit might think of my baptism, I long for him to come home. There are so many things I would like to make right with him. I failed him in so many ways."

Elsa stared. "You—make things right with Gerrit? You were his quiet, loving wife! He was the boor who didn't do his part and went his own selfish way!"

But Bettgen shook her head. "Some of it was my fault. I have been too selfish. I loved myself more than I loved him. I can see that now, and with Jesus in my heart, I would like a chance to try again…" Her voice broke.

Part Three
Gerrit Again

chapter twenty-one

Tricks up Their Sleeves

"It's just as I thought," grumbled Captain Piet to Gerrit. "This new Governor Requesens has marched an army up to Leiden. I figured that would be the Spaniards' next target. They have Haarlem, and they have Amsterdam. If they'd get Leiden yet too, our province of Holland would be cut in half. Hacked in two, like a frog under a hoe!"

Gerrit let out a low laugh. Usually he felt privileged in his friendship with the captain. For some reason unknown to him, Captain Piet often took Gerrit into his confidence. But Gerrit didn't always appreciate the coarse language Piet used.

"You say the Spanish army has reached Leiden already?" Gerrit questioned. Gazing across the sea, he could make out the dark line of the mainland. But of course he could not see the town of Leiden, for it lay miles inland.

"Yes, they've arrived with all their cannon, and are forming a wide ring around the city. At least that's what a fellow told me yesterday." Captain Piet's hands gripped the ship's railing. "Obviously they're settling in for a siege. They seem to have learned that violent attacks don't work with us Hollanders; we just fight back. So they plan to starve us out."

"I wish there were something we could do to help the town," Gerrit said. "Being it's land-locked, our ships can't go in."

"Our ships can't, but our men could." Captain Piet gave him a significant look. "I've been thinking that some of you should sneak in there behind the enemy lines. The Leideners will need all the encouragement they can get."

Locking eyes with his captain, Gerrit realized what he was hinting at. "You'd like me to go?"

"Very much. You're the right man for it. Also, we might send Jacob, and perhaps Pieke."

"What would our function be?"

"Oh, keeping a finger on the pulse of the town, if you know what I mean. Never let the pulse die down. Keep them upbeat. Remind them that Prince William and the Sea Beggars have a few tricks up their sleeves...providing the siege goes on long enough." He winked.

Gerrit knew what that wink meant, and he understood what Captain Piet meant by "tricks up their sleeves." But he didn't feel too optimistic about those tricks. Right now it was spring of 1574; autumn was still a long way off. Could Leiden hold out that long?

Captain Piet seemed to be reading his mind. "I know, there are months to go. That's why we need some men in there; men who will keep the town's mood bolstered. I'd give you letters of authorization. Will you go?"

Gerrit didn't hesitate. "Yes, I'll go. When do we leave? How do we get through the enemy lines?"

Captain Piet had his plans ready. Gathering the three designated men, he explained how they would be dropped on shore after dark. By morning they were to have reached a village where they would spend the daylight hours; and when darkness came again they would make a sprint for the enemy camp. Captain Piet knew of a secret entrance that would give them access through Leiden's city wall. Once inside, they were to immediately contact the burgomaster.

It was dangerous stuff. For the rest of the day, Gerrit tried not to think about that night's assignment. Instead he allowed his thoughts to stray down the coast, down, down to the Scheldt River, and upstream to a city called Antwerp.

He missed Bettgen. He had been away for almost a year now, and he still missed her. He had thought the memories would fade and he could melt seamlessly back into the Sea Beggars' life. But that was not how it worked. The ties were stronger than he'd realized.

Strangest of all, he even missed the children. He'd blamed them for driving him from home, blamed them for making his life miserable, and of course blamed Bettgen for bringing them into his life. But now in this rough existence of a pirate on the North Sea, he kept recalling Emily's silken yellow locks and Janneken's sweet smile and Henry's shy blue eyes.

It was ridiculous. Yet he'd tried in vain to get over it. And today, with this risky assignment looming over him, it was easier to think back home than to think ahead.

Other thoughts bothered him as well. These too he tried to push away, but they persisted. He could easily get killed, sometime in the next few days. What then? Was it true, as his childhood memories told him, that judgment awaited?

If so, then Gerrit Lieven was not ready. He knew that with a certainty so stark it sent shivers through his soul.

In a way it was a relief when night came and he and his friends were put ashore. At least now his mind would be occupied with other things as he applied all his wits to survive this dangerous mission.

Everything went according to plan during the first twenty-four hours. They found the village, and by the next night they had reached the enemy encampment. Gerrit's heart pounded as rows of tents loomed out of the darkness ahead. Were all the soldiers asleep? What if there were dogs? Stealthily the three men crept through, expecting any minute to hear loud shouts or barking.

But they reached the city wall without incident, and also found the secret entrance. The worst obstacle of the entire mission was the burgomaster's ire at being roused from his sleep. Even that had dissipated by the next morning when he became aware of his visitors' good intentions.

The next few days held a routine that was very strange for Gerrit. Town meetings were hosted, and assurances handed out concerning the Sea Beggars' loyal support. Spare minutes were spent entering shops and engaging in conversation with as many people as possible. Always the message was the same: Don't give up! Stand fast! Stay loyal to the Prince of Orange!

On the second day Gerrit entered a weaver's shop. Greeting him courteously, the owner listened to his information. Just as Gerrit prepared to leave, he noticed a sign with the owner's name: Pieter Pruys. Instantly he remembered that Govert's family had originally lived in Leiden.

Motioning toward the sign, Gerrit asked casually, "You wouldn't be a relative of Govert Pruys?"

A light went on in the weaver's eyes. "I had a brother by that name."

"Did he and his family live here some years ago? Did they move to Amsterdam, then Antwerp?" Gerrit prompted.

Pieter was watching him intently. No doubt he wondered whether he could trust this man. "Yes. And at Antwerp he and his wife were taken by the Inquisition."

"So you knew. Did you also hear what became of the children?"

"Only that they were taken in by a Catholic family."

"Well, my wife is at home right now caring for those five children," Gerrit told him.

Pieter's mouth opened, then closed again. His hands trembled. Obviously he still wondered what he could safely say. "My brother's children," he finally said. "And you—you are with the Sea Beggars."

"Yes." Gerrit decided to come right out and ask him: "Are you Mennonite?"

"I am." Pieter's voice was barely above a whisper. "I believe you can be trusted."

Humbly, Gerrit replied, "I hope so."

"When you see the children again, tell them that you met me. And tell them…" His voice broke. "Tell them God is faithful."

"I'll try," Gerrit promised. What would this man think if he told him that he didn't even know whether he'd ever go back?

That night he lay in the burgomaster's spare bed, unable to sleep. Over and over, Pieter's words repeated themselves in his head: "God is faithful…God is faithful."

Dawn had barely come when the burgomaster's shrill voice roused him. "Gerrit! You won't believe what's happening. Come and see."

Groggily he left the room and joined the burgomaster at his window, which commanded a view beyond the city gates. Yesterday morning from this very window, Gerrit had seen rank upon rank of Spanish tents.

This morning only a few tents were left, and those few were being folded. Lines of soldiers, loaded carts, and cannons moved southward, away from the city.

"Are they leaving?" Gerrit asked incredulously.

"That's what it looks like," came the burgomaster's reply.

"Why would they do that? Their camp was barely set up. They'd just started digging trenches. This doesn't make sense!" Gerrit exclaimed.

"Maybe not, but it's happening. Right in front of our eyes."

Gerrit's eyes narrowed. "This must be a trick, a ploy to bring us out there into their trap."

chapter twenty-two

How Leiden Was Saved

The reason for the Spanish withdrawal quickly became known. The army was needed elsewhere. Prince William's brothers, Lodewyk and Henry, had raised an army in Germany and had marched to the Netherlands. Their intention was to attack Brussels, the Spanish capital in Flanders! No wonder Requesens had commanded the army to hasten back.

Gerrit and his friends decided they would return to the ship. On their way out of the city they passed the weaver's shop. Impulsively Gerrit asked, "Could you two wait a few minutes? I learned to know this Pieter Pruys, and would like to say good-bye."

Pieke shrugged good-naturedly. "I suppose we can stand it here for another few minutes. Though I can hardly wait to feel a ship's deck under my feet again."

At Pieter's door, Gerrit felt suddenly embarrassed. Why had he come? Still, he went in, and Pieter greeted him warmly. "It seems our city has been granted a reprieve."

"It may be only temporary," Gerrit warned. After an awkward pause he added, "I just wanted to let you know I'm leaving."

"I'm glad I learned to know you. And many thanks to your wife for keeping those children. If only we could have them," Pieter responded wistfully.

"Maybe someday." Walking out of the shop, Gerrit asked himself why he had said that. "Bettgen wouldn't have liked to hear it," he thought. "She's pretty fond of those children."

Back on board, Gerrit kept a close watch on Captain Piet's travel plans. Would the ship head down toward Antwerp? If it did, he realized he'd be greatly tempted to leave. He realized more than ever before that he had left a part of his heart in the little house near the docks.

But Antwerp did not seem to be part of Captain Piet's plans. In what seemed like an aimless fashion to Gerrit, he cruised around among Zealand's many islands. Whenever the ship put into dock, he would make inquiries about the battle over near the German border. Requesens' army had intercepted Lodewyk and Henry there; they fought for days, far from Brussels, the city Lodewyk had intended to attack.

Little by little the news trickled in. Lodewyk and Henry had been defeated. Both were killed in battle. Many of their hired soldiers had deserted them.

"We must keep a wary eye on the Spanish army," Captain Piet said to Gerrit. "Now that they've won the battle with Lodewyk, I have a feeling they'll come back up to finish off Leiden. The Prince thinks so too; I heard he is urging the folks at Leiden to lay in plenty of provisions and prepare for what could be another long siege."

Sumner came, and with it some news that made Gerrit tremble.

"The Spanish army is mutinying!" Captain Piet told him. "King Philip hasn't enough money to pay the soldiers, and they refuse to fight again until they have been paid. We know only too well what mutinying soldiers tend to do."

Gerrit nodded. "They go around robbing and plundering. Where are these soldiers, do you know?"

"Many places. I've heard some are in Antwerp." Captain Piet eyed him narrowly. "That's where your family is, right?"

Gerrit clenched his fists. "Is there any way we could go down there?"

Captain Piet shrugged. "Not very easily, no. Besides, what could you do?"

"Not much, I guess." Gerrit had never felt so helpless in his life. Maybe those wild soldiers were hurting Bettgen—or Janneken— or Emily. Why, Bettgen was alone in that small house with the children. Anything could happen.

He was on the verge of begging Captain Piet to take him down the coast when more news came. The siege of Leiden was being resumed! The Spanish army—apparently well-paid again—was back, and this time they set up camp in earnest. This time, word had it, they planned to stay until the city surrendered, or until everyone starved.

"We must go up the coast and be on standby!" declared Captain Piet. "I heard that Leiden did not heed the Prince's advice. They didn't lay in extra provisions. Before long that will be one hungry town." Loading their ships with provisions, the Sea Beggars hovered off the coast, waiting, waiting.

Waiting for what? For autumn rains and rising waters. Now that summer had waned, there was hope—hope that the "tricks up the sleeves" of the pirates could actually come into play.

Day by day, week by week, the situation in Leiden grew more desperate. There were rumors of people starving by the dozen. There were rumors of the plague, killing hundreds more with its stealthy illness.

"If only the rains would come! If only the waters would rise!" moaned Captain Piet.

Finally, toward the end of September, his wish came true. Rain fell in abundance and winds blew in the right direction. Water in rivers and canals rose higher and higher. The secret was out: the dikes had been opened! Cuts had been made in strategic places; now the rising waters flowed through, flooding the countryside. Pastures and plowed fields alike were drowned beneath the silver tide.

The Sea Beggars sailed inland as far as they could with their ships. But near Leiden the floodwaters were not very deep. Now the Beggars boarded flat-bottomed boats that could move in very little water.

The flood alone would have been enough to send the Spaniards packing. But the Sea Beggars' boats struck even more terror into their hearts. And the last straw came early one morning when a huge section of the town wall collapsed.

The Spanish army fled. One morning they were gone. And when a starving boy, the first to venture outside the walls, entered the deserted camp he found a steaming pot of delicious stew.

But all these stirring events were lost on Gerrit Lieven. Where was he? He lay in his bunk, sick with a fever. One minute he was cold, the next minute he was fiery hot. Pieke and Jacob were at their wits' end as they tried to care for him. They knew he was very sick, for even when they told him the news about Leiden's salvation, he barely responded.

Wringing his hands, Jacob went to Captain Piet. "We must get Gerrit off this ship. He will die if we don't. If we could find someone in Leiden who would care for him, he might survive."

"I know!" exclaimed Pieke. "Remember that weaver's shop, where Gerrit stopped to say good-bye? If that man has not starved to death, maybe he would care for Gerrit."

Captain Piet nodded. "That's what we will do. It's the only hope for Gerrit, I fear."

So they maneuvered the ship to a spot where they could weigh anchor. Gently lowering the sick man into a rowboat, they paddled through the gap in Leiden's wall and searched for the weaver's shop.

Putting his mouth close to Gerrit's ear, Jacob said, "We're going to lay you on this board and carry you to the weaver's shop. What did you say the man's name was? Pieter something? Pieter Pruys?"

Gerrit moaned and opened his eyes slightly. "Pieter," he whispered. His moans continued during the bumpy trip down the street.

There was the shop. Both men remembered it from the day when they left Leiden. Jacob knocked, and a man opened. "Are you Pieter Pruys?" Jacob asked. Back in June he had seen the man briefly. This one looked so thin and hollow-eyed.

"Yes, I am." Pieter's eyes went to the invalid on the plank. "Who do we have here? Is it—can it be Gerrit Lieven?"

"It surely is, and he is a very sick man. We think he will die if he remains on board ship. Hoping someone in Leiden would care for him, we remembered you."

"Bring him in," Pieter said without hesitation. Leading the three to a room back of the shop, he quickly explained things to his wife. "It's the man I told you about—the one who took in

Govert's children."

"Oh! Put him down here," she exclaimed, turning back the blanket on their bed.

Gerrit moaned once more as they laid him on the straw mattress. Then he went still, and his breath came more evenly.

"He seems more peaceful than he has for days," Pieke marveled. Turning to Pieter he asked, "And what can we bring you? Our ships are loaded."

"Food." Pieter sighed. "We really could use some food."

chapter twenty-three

The Parable of Leiden

It was all so strange, yet somehow familiar. That other time when he woke up he had found himself at his sister's place. This time, Gerrit had no idea where he was. The room was tiny and dark. Who was that woman by the table? Certainly not his sister.

"Water," he said through parched lips.

The woman's head jerked up. Without a word she dashed out of the room, and when she came back a man was with her. The man—yes, he looked familiar. But who was he?

Suddenly Gerrit knew. "Pieter," he said as the man held a cup to his lips. The water felt cool in his burning throat. "Pieter Pruys. But I thought I had left Leiden. I thought I was on the ship."

"You were, but you got very sick. So your friend brought you here to recover. They said they'll be back in two weeks or so, before the water goes down again. They want to see how you are by then," Pieter explained.

Gerrit pushed himself up on one elbow—or tried to. He soon fell back on the pillow. "The water!" he said excitedly. "Did it come? Could the Beggars sail in to the city?"

"Indeed. The dikes were opened. And the ships came in, sailing over the pastures, pretty as you please," Pieter told him with a smile.

"The Spanish army is gone?"

"They're gone," came Pieter's firm reply. "I doubt if anyone can persuade those soldiers to ever come back to a land that becomes water at the Prince's bidding."

"It worked, then." Gerrit lay back with satisfaction. He felt tired out. Sleep soon overtook him.

The days passed in a haze. When his fever left him he could think clearly. One morning he told Pieter, "I ran away from my wife and the children, you know. I am a wicked man."

"You ran away," Pieter repeated gravely. Then he added, "If you repent, God will forgive you."

Gerrit lay silent, thinking that over. "God will forgive you." It sounded so desirable, so peaceful. Could it be true? Could God forgive a man as sinful as he?

The next day Pieter had a question for him. "We had planned to hold a meeting here in our house early on Sunday morning. Now I'm wondering if it's all right with you if we have it."

Gerrit pulled himself upright. "I can sit now. Yes, you go ahead with your plans." He could tell that Pieter was surprised at his ready reply. Maybe Pieter had expected him to object because he was a Catholic. He explained, "I'm not a very good Catholic. Also—had I told you? I grew up in a Mennonite home."

"You did!" exclaimed Pieter. Soon the two of them were sharing memories of the early days, when elder Menno Simons used to travel among the churches of the Netherlands .

"Over the years I have tried to break loose from my heritage," Gerrit confided. "But I find it a hard thing to break loose from. So—part of me is looking forward to tomorrow's meeting."

"There is nothing more valuable than the pure Word of God," Pieter declared fervently.

Gerrit never learned the name of the minister who spoke early the next morning. But he never forgot the Bible verses upon which the message was centered. They were from a book called "The Revelation of Jesus Christ." The first one was, *Behold, I stand at the door, and knock: if any man hear my voice, and open the door, I will come in to him, and will sup with him, and he with me* (Rev. 3:20). And the other one was: *And he showed me a pure river of water of life, clear as crystal, proceeding out of the throne of God, and of the Lamb* (Rev. 22:1).

The minister began by reminding the small congregation that Jesus in His preaching days often used natural events to illustrate spiritual truths. "Today's message will no doubt remind you of last week's happenings here in Leiden. Though we want no part in any warlike actions, we still can't help but see a vivid picture of similar struggles in our own lives."

He went on to speak of the sin that holds us in bondage, encamping round our hearts like a besieging army. He spoke of the spiritual starvation experienced by hearts under such a siege. And he spoke of man's helplessness in combating this ever-present sin.

"But there is this great river of water of life flowing from the throne of God—the flow of redemption and salvation through the cross of Jesus Christ. This river is always ready, always waiting to enter and succor our hearts. It is Jesus, knocking on our heart's door, bringing the 'supper' of His sacrificed life to feed our souls.

"Will we open the dikes? Will we become contrite and repentant and broken-hearted, to allow the water of life a free flow? It is the only way to have peace—the 'peace on earth' promised by the angels on the day Jesus was born."

There was much more to the message, but it was the first part that remained with Gerrit. He saw in it a way opened where no way had been apparent to him before. Since his marriage to Bettgen he had tried and struggled to overcome the sin and selfishness of his nature. But he had seen little success. His weaknesses had broken the marriage down. He could see that now; and he also saw a glimmer of hope. Hope through Jesus Christ, with His Holy Spirit cleansing a man's life like a pure crystal river.

Gerrit knew he would soon be leaving the Pruys home. Yet before he left, he felt the need to learn many things. Could he bring himself to open up and share his questions with Pieter?

The urgency was great enough that he dared. He asked questions about Jesus, the One who knocks on the door of men's hearts. He needed reassurance about the vast scope of forgiveness flowing from Christ's sacrifice on the cross. He needed to confess, broken-heartedly, just how great his own sin was.

After that there were questions about baptism, and about the life that must result when a heart is opened to the Lord. There were also a few worried questions about the dangers of living such a life—the dangers of going against the Spanish Inquisition. Yet it was amazing how those questions seemed to grow smaller as his concept of God's grace grew larger.

"I don't know what Bettgen will think of me," Gerrit admitted with a shake of his head. "She also has a Mennonite heritage, you know. And there were times when she seemed curious about the possibility of pursuing it. But on the whole she is a fairly committed Catholic. She conscientiously goes to Mass, prays to the saints, that sort of thing."

"God is faithful," said Pieter, reiterating a phrase that seemed to be a favorite of his.

And when Jacob and Pieke appeared the next day to take him back to the ship, Gerrit left the Pruys home with those words ringing in his ears: "God is faithful."

Captain Piet gave Gerrit a royal welcome back to the ship. But Gerrit lost no time before asking a very important question. "How soon can we go to Antwerp?"

A frown creased Captain Piet's forehead. "I would like to say, 'never.' I don't want to lose you again, Gerrit, and I have a feeling I will lose you if I take you there."

Gerrit said nothing. He just remained standing in front of his captain, awaiting a fuller reply. He knew Piet had a soft heart.

"But I can't say, 'never,'" Captain Piet admitted. "So I might as well answer, 'Right away!'"

The ship could not go fast enough. The Scheldt's broad estuary could not appear soon enough for Gerrit Lieven. At last he was on the dock, and then making his way along the winding street.

The little house had a forsaken appearance. When Gerrit tried the door, it was locked. A peek into the window showed forlorn emptiness. Gerrit's heart hammered in his breast. Had those mutinying Spanish soldiers taken all that was dearest on earth to him?

A sudden idea renewed his hope. Of course. Elsa would not have allowed Bettgen to stay here alone with the children.

Turning on his heel, he strode toward Jorg's place. To the carriage house. From the position of the sun, lowering in the sky,

Gerrit guessed they might be at supper.

The sounds coming through those dilapidated walls swelled his heart with joy. Should he knock? Or just walk in?

Before he could make up his mind, he heard a shriek from the window. He recognized the voice. It was his wife's, and the shriek had been one of recognition and delight.

The door burst open. They all spilled out to meet him. All six of them, safe and sound. He exclaimed at how the children had grown. Whenever possible, though, his eyes were on Bettgen. Something about her had changed too. No, she hadn't grown—at least not physically. But Gerrit knew there was another sort of growing that can change a person. Spiritual growth. Why did he detect something of that sort in his wife?

He was soon to find out. Eager to relate all the happenings he had missed, Wouter blurted out, "Aunt Bettgen was baptized. Did you know that, Uncle Gerrit? We go to meetings."

Thunderstruck, Gerrit locked eyes with his wife. Yes, the smile he saw there told him it was true.

On his way home, Gerrit had planned an elaborate speech to tell Bettgen about his spiritual journey, and explain why he wanted to contact the brethren here in Antwerp. He was going to tell her the "parable of Leiden," about the dikes that needed to be broken to let in the crystal-clear stream, bringing the bread of life through the Lamb of God. He'd even planned to relate a dim memory of something similar his father once said, about God's "water of life" being boundless as the North Sea, yet we humans maintain dikes of sin that keep out the pure flow.

Suddenly, however, that explanation was unnecessary. All he said was, "Why Bettgen, you beat me to it!"

After the children were in bed they had hours of time to talk.

Each shared the spiritual pilgrimage that had brought them to this point. Each confessed the failures they longed to correct so their marriage could go forward on a better footing. "Jesus as our foundation—that will be the difference," Gerrit said. "I'm afraid the change will not be overnight or magical, though. As Pieter said to me, 'It takes daily hard work, daily giving up—daily dying with Christ—to live a life pleasing to Him."

"God is faithful," Bettgen breathed, and Gerrit marveled how God's Word was the same across provinces and countries, and from one heart to the other.

"We had a letter from Adriana last week," Bettgen told him. "Remember? She was married to my brother Hansken before he died. I had written to tell her of my baptism. She wrote back, mentioning the freedom experienced by the brethren up there in the Danzig area. Well, I knew I wouldn't even consider moving. But now..."

"Now we will definitely consider it," Gerrit said firmly. "I was thinking about that on the way home. These children have been orphaned once. We'll do what we can to keep them from being orphaned a second time."